SUMMER
OF CHOICES

CORNERSTONE BRETHREN CHURCH
AND MINISTRIES

Books in the Forever Friends series

SUMMER OF CHOICES

Lynn Craig

OLIVER
NELSON

THOMAS NELSON PUBLISHERS
Nashville • Atlanta • London • Vancouver

Published in Nashville, Tennessee, by Thomas Nelson, Inc., Publishers, and distributed in Canada by Word Communications, Ltd., Richmond, British Columbia.

The Bible version used in this publication is THE NEW KING JAMES VERSION. Copyright © 1979, 1980, 1982, Thomas Nelson, Inc., Publishers.

Library of Congress Cataloging-in-Publication Data

Craig, Lynn.
    Summer of choices / Lynn Craig.
      p. cm. — (Forever friends series : bk. 3)
    Summary: Katelyn keeps a journal of Forever Friends club summer activities, including their preparations for a Labor Day frisbee tournament to earn money to refurbish the town park.
    ISBN 0-8407-9241-7 (pbk.)
    [1. Diaries—Fiction. 2. Clubs—Fiction.
3. Friendship—Fiction. 4. Christian life—Fiction.]
I. Title. II. Series: Craig, Lynn. Forever friends series : bk. 3.
PZ7.C84426Su 1994
[Fic]—dc20   94–4504
                                     CIP
                                     AC

Printed in the United States of America.
1 2 3 4 5 6 — 99 98 97 96 95 94

To

Amy and Mary

Chapter One

Wrongs Made Right

Wednesday
8 P.M.

*K*iersten Elizabeth Marie Weber!

"Kiersten Elizabeth Marie Weber!"

I knew that I was yelling, dear Journal, and that my face was probably crimson—which is not its most becoming color—but I really didn't care. I was furious.

You see, dear Journal, I had just hung up from talking to Kimber. She wasn't angry, but I could tell she was upset. (It isn't like Kimber to get angry. She's much too sweet and easygoing for that. She does get hurt and upset, though. Don't we all!)

Anyway . . . all morning, it seems . . . Mari, her little sister, had taunted her by puckering her lips and making little smooching sounds. Not when her parents could see what she was doing, of course, but sort of behind their backs—just teasing and then running away. I can just imagine how infuriating that would be!

Kimber said she finally had chased Mari into a corner and grabbed her and demanded to know how she knew about the kiss. Mari, she said, had just shrugged her shoulders and smiled innocently.

In the afternoon, Mari's tactic had switched. She'd smile and say sweetly—more like syrup, in Kimber's words—"Dennis and Kimber. Kimber and Dennis." Maddening! It was driving Kimber nuts. And to make matters worse, Kimber couldn't get Mari to stop . . . she couldn't find out how Mari knew . . . and she couldn't get Mari to promise that she wouldn't tell anybody. It was at that point that Kimber called me. Luckily, I'm not working at The Wonderful Life Shop this week—since Mrs. Miller is out of town with Trish for a few days, Aunt Beverly suggested I take the week off and stay home with Kiersten.

"If that was Kiersten," I said on the phone to Kimber, "I'd probably demand a family court tickle."

"A what?" she said.

"A family court tickle," I repeated. "You know, like a court-martial or a court date. It's something Mom came up with when we were both little—in fact, we started them when Kiersten was just a

2

toddler and was always hanging around trying to copy everything I did."

"A family court tickle? How's it work?" Kimber asked.

"Well, the person who is being bugged—which is you—gets permission from a parent to catch and tickle the person who is doing the bugging, which would be Mari. You get to tickle her as much as you can. But the rules are that she can also try to defend herself by tickling you back."

"And this does some good?" Kimber asked with a big dose of skepticism in her voice.

"Oh, sure!" I said, trying my best to help Kimber feel better. "The point is, you both end up laughing so hard that you're exhausted, and the person who has been feeling bugged doesn't feel bugged anymore, and the person who has been doing the bugging usually doesn't feel like pestering anymore, either."

"Well, it m-i-g-h-t work," Kimber said hesitantly.

"The only time I've seen it *not* work," I said, "is if a person isn't ticklish!"

"That *would* put a damper on things," admitted Kimber, sounding much more light-hearted.

"Kiersten is more ticklish than I am so this usually works to my advantage. In fact, I remember a time," I said . . . and that's when the idea hit me, *Kiersten is the one who told Mari about the kiss!*

"Are you still there?" Kimber said. I obviously had trailed off into silence and her words jolted me back to the phone.

"Yes, and I'm afraid this may be all my fault, Kimber," I said.

"What do you mean?" she said.

"Well, there's a distinct possibility that Kiersten is the one who told Mari."

"But how would Kiersten know?" asked Kimber. "You didn't tell her, did you? You promised!"

"No, I didn't tell her," I said. "At least not intentionally or directly. But you know that I keep a journal and write in it as often as I can, right?"

"Of course. You even gave me a journal as a graduation present, remember?"

"That's right. I'm not thinking with all my computer chips active," I said.

"Computer chips?" said Kimber with a little laugh. "You *have* been hanging around Jon too much lately!"

"You're right," I chuckled. "That's one of his latest phrases. Anyway . . . as I was saying . . . I wrote about your kiss in my journal. After all, it's one of the most exciting things that's happened this summer."

"*The* most exciting," said Kimber with a sigh.

4

"And . . . ," I went on, "Kiersten just may have found my journal."

"Oh, no," sighed Kimber. I could see her in my mind's eye, pulling her pillow over her head.

"'Oh, no' is right," I said. "If she knows about your kiss and has told Mari about it, then she knows lots of other things I'd just as soon she not know about. Don't worry, Kimber. I'll get to the bottom of this and make sure that Kiersten keeps her mouth shut. If there's one thing that's sacred besides the Bible, it's got to be secrets!"

"I hope she'll keep quiet," said Kimber. "I'd hate for any of this to get back to Dennis. It would just be too . . ."

"Mortifying!" I said, finishing her sentence for her. "Don't think about it. I'm going to hang up right now and deal with this."

After I hung up the phone, I called for Kiersten but I couldn't find her anywhere. *Just like her to disappear when trouble is about to come her way,* I thought. I looked everywhere. And, as you can imagine, the more I looked and *didn't* find her, the angrier and more upset I got.

When I first started writing things down— such as an entry in a diary, or a story in a note-book—Kiersten and I shared the same bedroom. That was back in Eagle Point. Kiersten somehow always found a way to find what I had written. It was tough to find a good hiding place, especially in one room! Most of the time, I didn't mind. Kiersten really liked the little stories I wrote so it was even a compliment that she looked so hard to see if I had written anything new.

But then when I started putting down things that were really important to me—some of my dreams and goals, and especially some of my deepest feelings, like the way I felt after Mom died, or the way I wished I could have a boyfriend like some of my other friends, or the way I felt when Dad first told us that we were moving to Collinsville—I didn't like it that Kiersten always found my diaries. I felt as if she'd invaded my privacy, which, of course, she had!

It's not that I have ever really wanted to keep secrets from Kiersten. She's my little sister and ninety-nine percent of the time, I adore her. She's one of the funniest, spunkiest, most outgoing girls I've ever met. Gramma Weber calls her a "sunny bunny," a phrase I've always loved. I'd do just about anything for Kiersten, and in the right time and place, I can't imagine that I'd refuse to answer any of her questions or keep from telling her anything that I thought she was old enough to hear. Still . . . it's one thing to voluntarily tell someone your feelings. It's another thing for a person to unearth your feelings without your ever having given them permission to dig in your garden! (Wow, how's that, dear Journal, for a turn of phrase? Aunt Beverly taught me last week about "turning a phrase"! It's something every writer should try to do, I think.)

The worst part of all this is that Kiersten not only snooped, but she *told*. That's what really made me mad, and madder, and madder still. By the time I finally found her—just quietly playing with her dolls up in the big old sycamore tree in the backyard, carefree and content in pure Kiersten style—I was just plain furious.

"What do you want?" said Kiersten from her lofty perch.

"Come down here right now," I demanded.

"Are you angry?" she asked innocently. Which only made me even more angry, if that was possible.

"Yes, I am," I said.

"Then I think I'll stay up here," she said. "At least until you tell me why you're so upset."

"I'm upset because you've been in my journal, haven't you?"

"No, I have not," she said, very decisively.

"Are you lying to me, Kiersten Elizabeth Marie Weber?" I demanded again. If there's one thing I've always been able to count on, it's that Kiersten doesn't seem to know how to lie—at least not without giving herself away completely. When she lies, she can't hold a straight face. If you wait just a second or two, she starts giggling.

"No, I'm not lying. And I haven't been in your

journals. I don't even know where you're hiding them now."

I waited a few seconds. There were no giggles. *Could I have miscalculated?*

"Then how did Mari know about Dennis kissing Kimber?" I asked in my best prosecuting-lawyer style.

"Dennis kissed Kimber?" Kiersten said. Her eyes got big as saucers. The evidence was plain for any jury to see. Kiersten *hadn't* been lying—and I had just blown it.

"It was just a joke," I said, trying desperately to cover my tracks.

"The kiss was a joke, or your telling me was a joke?" asked Kiersten, gathering up her dolls and preparing to come down from her safe haven to learn more.

"Neither one," I said.

"Then it was a *real* kiss?" she asked, still wide-eyed.

"Just forget it," I said. "It's none of your business."

"Then why were you so mad at me if it was none of my business?"

She had me there.

"Kiersten," I said. "I've made a big mistake. I've just accused you of doing something that you didn't do. I'm sorry about that. But now I've told you something I had promised I'd never tell a soul.

Please promise me right here and now that you won't tell *anybody* about this—not Mari, not anybody."

"Doesn't Mari already know?" she asked.

"Why do you say that?"

"Well, you asked me if I was the one who told Mari, so Mari must know."

About that time, I was beginning to think that this little sister was getting too big and too smart.

"Mari *thinks* she knows," I said. "But it's really none of her business. In fact, it's not my business either. And it's not your business. It's something that should be private between Kimber and Dennis."

"Then how come you know?" Kiersten asked.

"Well . . . because I'm Kimber's friend and she told me, and she asked me not to tell anybody," I said, sitting down on the quilt with Kiersten. "Promise me you won't tell."

"Why should I promise? Kimber didn't ask me not to tell." I couldn't tell if Kiersti was trying to totally unravel me or if she was asking an honest question.

"Because you're Kimber's friend, aren't you?" I asked.

"Yes," she said.

"Well, a friend might know another friend's secrets, but they don't tell the secrets," I said. (I'm not sure where those words came from, but I was very grateful they came. Aunt Beverly once told me that the Holy Spirit sometimes gives us just the right words to say in difficult situations. I think that must be what happened.)

Kiersten was thoughtful for a few seconds. I could see that she was mulling over what I had said as she straightened her dolls around her on the old quilt that she had left on the ground under the tree.

"OK," she finally said, "I promise."

"Not a word?" I said.

"No," she replied. "I promise. But only because I'm Kimber's friend." I leaned over to give her a big hug but Kiersten pulled away.

"What?" I asked.

"Next time don't get so mad at me."

"You're right," I said. "I should have made sure I had my facts straight."

"It's OK," she said. And then she leaned over and gave me a hug.

At that point, who should walk through the back gate but Jon.

"What are you girls up to?" he asked with his usual grin. "Oh," he added, stopping short, "dolls." He pretended to back off with his hands raised in apology. "Sorry, they're out of my league."

"Actually," I said, "we were just having a good heart-to-heart sisterly type conversation."

"What about?" Jon asked, looking first at me and then at Kiersti.

"I can't tell," we both said at the same time.

"Why not?" asked Jon.

"It's a secret!" we both said again, just at the same time, giggling even as we did.

"Am I hearing things in stereo?" asked Jon, looking up toward the sky and shaking his head as if to clear his ears.

"Come on into the house," I said. "I was just getting ready to make some old-fashioned lemonade."

"You know," added Kiersten with a tease in her voice, "the kind that comes out of a carton from the store."

"It's my favorite," said Jon as he followed me into the kitchen. "Do you want me to bring you a glass, Kiersten?"

"No thanks," she said. She was already back playing with her dolls, even before we got inside.

As I poured Jon a big glass of lemonade, he said, "Since our next club meeting is tomorrow night, I thought I'd better come over this afternoon and talk to you about my idea for a project."

"Great!" I said. "You're about the best vice-president a president could ever have."

"Right," said Jon, apparently thinking I was joking.

"No, I mean it," I said. "You've got great ideas—

and even better, you're willing to share them. Maybe you should be president."

"No way," said Jon. "Then you're talking administration—which tends to mean planning and phone calls and making sure everybody is thinking along the same lines. That's you, not me."

"Well, at least we're a team," I said.

"I hope so," said Jon.

There was a little something in his voice I wasn't sure I wanted to pursue, so I quickly said as I sat down across from him at the kitchen bar, "So, what's the idea?"

"Everybody likes Frisbees, right?" Jon asked. "And just about everybody can throw a Frisbee, right?"

"Sure," I said. "At least everybody I know."

"So . . . we could make a little golf course at the park that was just for Frisbees, and call it Frisbee golf."

"You mean dig holes in the park big enough for Frisbees to go into?"

"No . . . we could use bushel baskets," said Jon. "In fact, that's where I got the idea. Your grandpa and dad were unloading some things into the store last week and I saw them unload some bushel baskets. One of the clerks pretended to throw paper into one of them as if it were a basketball hoop, and that's when the idea hit me."

"I like it," I said. "So the idea is to build a Frisbee golf course at the park."

"That's just part of it," said Jon. "I don't know that the city leaders would go for a permanent Frisbee golf course at the park—the baskets would probably rot in the rain and snow, and would need replacing and all. What I had in mind was a Frisbee golf tournament to raise money. People would pay a fee to play the course and then we could use the money for a good cause."

"And I know just what that cause might be!" I said. "I was at the park with Kiersten just yesterday. Even though she's ten, she still loves to go down the slide and play on the equipment in the park. A lot of it has paint that's worn off. And the benches in the park could use a new coat of paint, too."

"Good idea!" said Jon. "And if there was any money left over, we might be able to plant a tree or a few new bushes, too."

"Fabulous," I said. "So how would a tournament like this work?"

"Well, the only ones I know about are the golf tourneys I've been to with my dad. The players pay a fee to enter the tournament and then the winner gets part of the money for a prize—or sometimes they just get a trophy or certificate, or maybe a piece of golf equipment."

"Do you think we should have age levels?"

"That would be good. That way, anybody could play."

"And we might charge just a quarter or something for practice rounds so people could get used to the course."

"And then maybe charge according to your age for the actual tournament."

The ideas were really flowing!

"Jon, I think this is a *wonderful* idea! I'm sure everybody else will think so, too. And if we're all in agreement, we might even be able to share this idea with the City Council. Aunt Beverly told me they are having a meeting next week."

"Is your Aunt Beverly on the City Council?" Jon asked.

"No, but she has an idea to propose to them, so she's going to the meeting. She invited me to go along to see what a council meeting is like. I've never been to one before. Anyway, I can see what she thinks about our having a chance to ask about this idea."

"Good move," said Jon. "You might want to talk to her even before our meeting in case there's some kind of agenda we need to get ourselves on. We could always back out."

"I'll call her tonight after she's had a chance to get home from the shop."

"Well, actually," said Jon, "I think she's meeting someone for dinner right after work."

"Anybody I know?" I asked, teasing him.

"Yes, actually," said Jon. "But it's no big deal. They've invited me to tag along."

"Your father asked *you* to go along on a date with Aunt Beverly?" I said. "Some date."

"I'm not sure it's really a date," said Jon. "Just dinner. In fact, it sounds more like a meeting of some kind. Dad said your Aunt Beverly wanted to talk to us about a business idea she has."

I knew in an instant *exactly* what Aunt Beverly had in mind, but I didn't say anything. I don't want Jon to think we talk about everything, even though we do. I simply said, "Well, if it's a business idea and it involves Aunt Beverly, you can be sure it's going to be a success."

"That's what Dad said."

"He did?"

"Yeah," said Jon, helping himself to the cookie jar I had shoved over in his direction. "He thinks she's one outstanding businesswoman."

"Is that all he thinks?" I asked, almost wishing I hadn't opened my mouth as soon as I had asked the question.

"I think he thinks more than that," said Jon with a grin. "But I'd better not get myself into hot water here."

"You're right," I said. "We might be better off not knowing."

15

"Do you think Trish will be back by tomorrow night?" Jon asked.

"I don't know. Mrs. Miller called Dad last night and I heard him say, 'Take all the time you need,' so it didn't sound to me as if they were going to be back real soon. I can ask him tonight."

"You'd better make a list of all the things you have to ask," Jon teased.

"Speaking of lists, I've got this list of things to get ready for dinner. Do you mind if I start doing some of those things while we talk?"

"Not at all," said Jon. "I love to watch a woman work."

"In that case, here," I said, handing him a potato peeler and reaching into the pantry cupboard to get out a sack of potatoes.

"Actually, this is one of my specialties," said Jon. He didn't seem to mind at all helping me with the potatoes while I started to defloss some ears of corn.

As we worked, I asked Jon, "Do you think we need to wait to get Trish's input before we go ahead with your idea for a Frisbee golf tournament?"

"No," said Jon. "I was just wondering when she's going to be back."

"Oh," I said. *Could Jon be interested in Trish as more than a friend?* Something about that idea almost made me panic a little.

"Actually," said Jon, "I wasn't the one who was

really wondering. Ford has asked me twice when I think she's going to be back."

"Ford?" I asked. "And Trish?" I felt relieved—I'm not sure why.

"Who knows?" said Jon with a grin. "He seems to enjoy talking about her quite a bit. It really upset him that she rode off to Fruitvale on her bike all by herself. For a while there I couldn't tell if he was mad or worried."

"I think we all felt that way," I sighed. "There hasn't been an hour these last two days that I haven't thought of Trish. Maybe we can come up with an idea tomorrow night about what we can do to let Trish know how worried we were—if and when she gets back to Collinsville."

"Do you think there's a chance she won't come back to Collinsville?" Jon asked.

"Who knows? Dad said he wouldn't be surprised if Trish's parents returned and Trish stayed in Fruitvale."

"Well, that probably would be the best thing," said Jon. "But I know one guy who would be more than a little disappointed."

"You seem to know quite a bit," I said. "What else do you know?"

"Oh, not much," said Jon. "I know Dennis finally got up his nerve to kiss Kimber."

"You know about that?" I asked. *Did everybody know?*

"Yeah. Dennis was pretty high about it."

"Dennis? Dennis told you?" I asked.

"Yeah," Jon admitted. "Are we gossiping?"

"Probably," I said, but went right on with my next question anyway. "What did he say?"

"Not much, actually," said Jon. "He stopped by Ford's yesterday and Ford was showing us how to play his new game called 'The Find'—it's a neat new game about archaeology—anyway, he just said that he finally got a real birthday kiss and that it was great."

"Is that all he said?" I asked. Guys just don't seem to go for the details like we girls do.

"Pretty much."

"And what else do you know, Mr. Jon Weaver?" I asked.

"That I'm going to be late meeting Dad and your Aunt Beverly if I don't leave thirty seconds ago."

And before I knew it, he was out the door.

I made sure Kiersti was still outside and that Jon was well down the street—running in his slow loping kind of jog—before I called Kimber.

"It wasn't Kiersten," I said.

"I know," said Kimber. "It was pure Mari."

"What do you mean?"

"She saw us in the car from her bedroom window. She said she had been looking out at the stars when she saw us pull up."

"Not much you can do about that," I said.

"Well, I tickled her," said Kimber, laughing a little.

"I should go do that to Kiersten," I said. "I was pretty mad at her—and all for no reason."

"Does Kiersti know?"

"Yeah. I really messed up." I told Kimber what had happened, giving her a line-by-line account of our conversation. "Do you think she'll keep her promise?" Kimber asked when I was finished.

"I think so. Kiersten is pretty good with secrets and telling the truth."

"I'd just hate for anything to get back to Dennis. I don't want him to think I've been telling everybody what happened."

"Well, as a matter of fact," I said, "I wouldn't worry about that too much if I were you."

"What do you mean?" she said. And I launched into a second line-by-line replay of the conversation I had with Jon.

Kimber just giggled and sighed, and then giggled and sighed again, all the way through it. "So," I said in concluding my account of what Jon said, "he thinks it was wonderful and you think it was wonderful, so . . ."

"It was wonderful!" she said.

As for me . . . the most wonderful part of today is that I can now go to sleep—yikes, it's almost midnight—knowing that I'm not at odds with anybody. Things are OK with Kimber. They're OK with Kiersti. They're OK with Jon . . . and Dad . . . and Grandpa . . . and Aunt Beverly . . . and with everybody in Collinsville as far as I know. Still, it was a rather topsy-turvy afternoon. Dad would probably have called it "rough water." It felt like that. My stomach and nerves probably couldn't take too much of that in a week.

I can't help but wonder, though . . . what will happen if and when Trish returns? We need to do something special for her.

Chapter Two

Decisions

I can hardly believe it! Nine days have gone by since I've written in you, dear Journal. I think that must be a record—and not one I'm particularly happy about. The days have been so busy I've hardly known which way to turn first. Which means, of course, that I hardly know what to write about first.

The biggest news is that Trish is coming back to Collinsville this weekend, and she's going to stay for the rest of the summer! We weren't so sure that was going to happen until just yesterday. Mrs. Miller came back last Sunday. Trish's parents had returned from their vacation and Mrs. Miller said they decided it would be good for them to spend some time with Trish. So Mrs. Miller came back to Collinsville without her.

We were really sad that Trish didn't come with her. On the other hand, we all think it's great that Trish can be with her parents. Mrs. Miller seemed a little distracted all week. One night she completely forgot to make gravy for the mashed potatoes. She even put her purse in the refrigerator by mistake one morning. We teased her about it for two days! I could tell she was concerned about Trish. Her concern made me more concerned than I might otherwise have been.

Then yesterday morning Mrs. Miller arrived at our house with a big smile on her face and when I asked her what was making her so happy, she said, "My prayer has been answered, Katelyn! Trish is coming back this weekend to spend the rest of the summer." We talked a little more about it and it seems that this time, it's Trish's idea to come. She'll probably be more content here for a few weeks now that it's her idea. I hope so. She always seemed just a little restless and uneasy.

Anyway . . . we're all excited that she's coming back and we have a big surprise "welcome back" party planned for tomorrow night. There's lots still to do—we each have "chores" to do for the party. Jon and Ford are making a banner on Ford's computer. And Libby and I are doing the refreshments, with a little help from Mrs. Miller, too. Kimber and Dennis are making a special fruit punch, and Julio is in charge of photography (including getting some film for his camera). And we're all meeting at Baker's Craft and Hobby Store at ten o'clock to buy supplies to make Trish a friendship bracelet. But more on that later. That really goes back to our last FF meeting, which we decided last week could now stand for "Friends and Frisbees!"—at least that's what it can mean for a few weeks.

Everybody loved Jon's idea about a Frisbee tournament to raise money to fix up some of the park equipment. Julio suggested that the grand prize for the winner be a Frisbee specially painted by Kimber—with the tournament name and date on it, and a design of Kimber's choice. Kimber agreed, of course, although I think she was a bit overwhelmed that everybody thought she could make a really professional-looking award. I don't have any doubt that she can. She's a good artist.

The group authorized—we guessed that "authorized" was the word we should use for our formal club minutes—that Jon and I should try to go to the next City Council meeting with our idea, and that if the Council approved of it, we would make posters announcing the tournament, design the course, collect the money, and do the painting. In a nutshell, we'd do all the work! Still, it sounded like good fun to all of us, and Linda pointed out that we're all probably going to get very good at throwing Frisbees before the summer is over!

Well . . . I also talked to Aunt Beverly about

the City Council meeting, and the long and the short of it is, the meeting was last Tuesday night. Jon and I were scrambling over the weekend to get all of our ideas down on paper in a way that was easy for someone to understand at a quick glance what it is that we want to do. Aunt Beverly said that was important because the Council doesn't like to take a lot of time with any one item on its agenda.

As part of our research, Jon and I went over to the park last Sunday afternoon and scoped it all out. We decided that we should probably limit the number of "holes" to nine, and we sort of mapped out the park and a plan for where the bushel baskets and the tee-off spots should go. It's one thing to go by or through a park just for fun. It's another thing to actually think about how a park is laid out and where all the trees and bushes and walkways are. I have a whole new conception of our park!

We showed our plan to Aunt Beverly and Mr. Clark Weaver when we got back to Jon's house (Aunt Beverly was there, which was a fun surprise . . . she hadn't told me!) and Aunt Beverly suggested that we also put on our map a place where local merchants or other community clubs might come and set up little booths to sell hot dogs and soft drinks and other types of food to the people who are in the tournament. Great idea!

On Tuesday, Jon and I dressed up a little (out of jeans and shorts and into church-style clothes) and went to the City Council meeting. That was a first for me! The place where they meet is a little auditorium toward the back of City Hall.

The City Hall in Collinsville is my favorite building. It's very formal looking and it just may be the oldest building in town—I should ask Grandpa Stone about that. It's the only three-story building in town, and since it sits on a little hill at the end of the main plaza, it sort of dominates the plaza and makes the entire downtown area seem pretty formal and serious. The building is made of red brick with white pillars and a big front veranda. The top of the building has a little dome, just like the state capitol. Flags always fly in front of the building. All in all, it's just the way a city hall should look, as far as I'm concerned.

The auditorium is on the main floor, and even though it's small, it has a tiered floor just like the small theater where plays are held in Eagle Point. There are probably about sixty seats in the audience part of the auditorium, and then up on the stage area, there's a big half-circle-shaped desk for the council members to sit behind. The mayor sits in the middle and the other six council members sit on either side of him—three to his right, and three to his left. Each person has a name plate in front of him. Two other people also sit at the main desk—on either end. One is the city manager and the other is the city attorney. The official seal of Collinsville is on the wall behind the mayor's seat and on either side of it are the names of all the official community service clubs and organizations, including the Chamber of Commerce. Jon reminded me that we need to see about getting a seal designed for the FF Club so we can have it mounted with the other seals. On either side of the stage area are flags—our state flag and the American flag. It's a pretty formal room—all done in wood and shades of navy blue and beige. Very impressive.

The night we were there, several reports were given as a part of the "new business" of the meeting. Miss Jones, president of the Collinsville Chamber of Commerce, gave a report on behalf of the Bridge to Benton committee. She announced that a committee had been put together to come up with a plan to encourage more people to drive out from Benton to shop at Collinsville, and she described for the Council their goals and budget and the names of the people on the committee. Jon and I are supposed to be part of that committee—along with Libby. It was a little strange to hear our names being read while we sat there in the audience.

Aunt Beverly also gave a report on her Chamber of Commerce committee, which is the City

Beautification Committee. She announced an official "Sprucing Up Collinsville" campaign that is going to start this fall with the planting of lots of miniature spruce trees in big terra cotta pots along Main Street. The advantage of the evergreens is that they will beautify the downtown area, not shed leaves, and they can be decorated for the holiday season. She showed a painting that an architect had made for the committee. One look convinced me: the main street of Collinsville is going to look great!

And then came time for Jon and me to make our presentation. We really didn't have time to get nervous—we were listening so closely to what Miss Jones and Aunt Beverly had to say, we almost forgot we were next! Anyway, I gave a brief introduction and then Jon described the details of the tournament. Right away, everybody on the City Council seemed to jump in with more suggestions of their own. The idea was a hit!

A big discussion resulted and when it was all over, here's what had been decided:

First, the park course is going to be set up the first of August and people will have all of August to practice. The City Council thought it would be too difficult to have someone at the park all the time to collect money from people for each round of Frisbee they played. Instead, they suggested an honor system—that we put collection containers at several stores, including Stone's Hardware and McGreggor's, and then put a big article in the local community paper, *The Collinsville Press*, about the tournament and the honor system, and so forth. People would voluntarily pay for their practice rounds and a little sign at the course would remind them to make a donation.

Second, the City Council thought the tournament should be part of the city's Labor Day celebration. There's a big barbecue and variety show already scheduled for that day, and a fun fair is going to be held on the parking lot of the high school, which is just across the street from the park. The City Council thought it was a great idea for people to set up food booths on one edge of the park—they could serve both the tournament players and the people going to the fun fair. Labor Day is apparently a big day here in Collinsville. Both Jon and I were a bit surprised by that. We've never lived in towns where Labor Day was celebrated so much.

At first, Jon and I weren't sure we liked the idea about the tournament being part of the Labor Day activities. I guess we thought it might become just one more thing to do, and not as many people would enter the tournament. The City Council members convinced us that we'd actually have *more* people since families would be back from their summer vacations. Miss Jones asked to speak and she said she thought the tournament would be a great draw even for people from Benton and that perhaps her committee could come up with a few quick ideas for promoting the entire day's activities as a fun outing for Benton families.

Our other concern was that this was intended to be a fund-raiser so we could raise money to buy paint to fix up the park. Since school starts the day after Labor Day, we couldn't see how we would have enough time to paint the park equipment. The City Council came up with a great plan—they're going to advance us the money to buy paint and the bushel baskets, and to make posters and collection containers. And then, as money comes in, they'll be reimbursed. As part of the sign at the Frisbee course's first "tee-off" spot, we're going to have a thermometer-style design to show how much money has been raised. And . . . we're going to paint *part* of the park equipment and benches as we go along. The mayor said he thought that would be an incentive for people to give—plus, they'd be able to see that what they were putting into the containers was being used for the intended purpose. We all liked that idea, and it solved the problem. We'll be able to start painting as soon as we set up the course.

One of the council members asked what we were planning to do with any money that we might raise beyond the cost of supplies. Frankly,

Jon and I hadn't thought there would be any money left over after we bought paint and bushes or a tree. The Council voted that we could keep any "profits" from the tournament (after reimbursing the City Council) as part of our FF Club funds. Wow! Talk about incentive. We never really discussed *making* money on the tournament. There are probably lots of things we could think about doing.

The very next afternoon—Wednesday—Jon and I were invited to come to *The Collinsville Press* for an interview about the tournament. They've promised to write up a big article for next week's paper and they even took pictures of Jon and me with our Frisbees.

Given all that had happened, we decided to call an emergency meeting of the FF Club for last night so that we could get started on what we need to do for the tournament. We really made serious plans and assignments. Julio and Jon are going to be in charge of the course—getting the baskets, deciding exactly where they are going, and so forth. We decided that we could mark the tee-off spots with croquet wickets. Kimber and Libby are going to work on the sign at the beginning of the course and also the posters. Ford is going to make the containers that will go in the various stores for contributions. I'm supposed to work on more publicity and contact the stores and make a plan for keeping track of the money. We're all going to be busy! It feels good, though, to be doing something with this summer and not just goofing off.

Now, back to Trish. After we had talked about the first Collinsville Frisbee Tournament at our meeting a week ago, we got into a conversation about Trish. I was a little surprised at all of the feelings people had. Libby was upset, but also a little angry. She felt that Trish had lied to her about where she was going. She also felt a little used—that Trish had conned her into filling in for her as a waitress at Tony's Pizza Parlor.

"When she gets b-b-back, I'm going to give her a p-p-piece of my mind," Libby said. "A b-b-big piece!"

I don't think I've ever seen Libby quite so put out with anybody or anything. She usually just goes along with the flow of what is being said or decided, and although she can feel hurt, I've never seen her angry before. It only makes her stuttering worse, too.

Kimber said, "I'm not angry as much as I am sad. I thought we were better friends than for her to up and leave town without even so much as a word to any of us. That's not what friends do."

"Maybe Trish doesn't know how to be a friend," Jon said, with half a question in his voice. "She may never have had friends like us who really care."

"That's right," Julio added. "After all, if she had

31

asked any one of us to go with her, we just might have gone along for the ride."

"I think she was scared," said Ford, "and homesick, too. She probably knew it wasn't the *right* thing to do, but when you miss someone a lot, you tend to do things that don't always make sense." I could feel Jon looking at me while Ford was talking, to see if I was going to give away the fact that I know how much Ford likes Trish, but I didn't even raise an eyebrow. Jon seemed relieved I didn't say anything.

"Well," said Libby, "it's probably a g-g-good thing if I don't see her right when she gets b-b-back."

"Yeah," said Julio, "you'd better have a chance to chill out a little first."

"Do you think I'm w-w-wrong about the way I f-f-feel?" asked Libby. Frankly, I could see Libby's point. Trish had asked Libby to take her job at Tony's for just a few days while she and her grandmother went on a little vacation. She didn't say anything about not coming back, or about where she was really going. And she *had* lied about the vacation.

Linda said, "I don't know Trish all that well, but I think you may be just a little too hard on her, Libby. She must have been pretty desperate to do what she did. Her parents are having problems and she doesn't know what's going on or what they are going to decide about staying married—I'd be a nervous wreck if that was happening in my family."

"How do you know all that?" asked Dennis.

"Trish told me while we were riding to Benton. I asked her if her parents were going to be at the finish line and she told me about staying with her grandmother and why she was there."

Kimber and Libby both caught my eye. I think we were all a little surprised that Trish had never really opened up to any of us about that, but had to Linda—whom she had known only a few weeks.

"Talking about her folks like that is probably what made her really want to see them again," I said.

"Yeah," said Julio, "It explains why she just up and left."

"I'm not sure any of us can really tell how Trish felt, or how she feels," said Ford. "Here we all are, talking about her and she's not here to say anything for herself."

"Ford's right, I think," said Jon.

"The thing we need to decide is what we are going to do and how we're going to act when she gets back," said Kimber.

"Except for Libby," said Dennis. "She already knows!"

At that Libby seemed to soften some. "Oh, I'm just blowing off s-s-steam," she said. "By the time she comes b-b-back, I'm going to be as g-g-glad as any of you to s-s-see her."

"When is she coming back?" asked Ford.

"Nobody knows," I said. "Mrs. Miller doesn't even know. In fact, she may not ever come back—at least for more than a day or two to visit her grandmother."

"Really?" said Kimber.

"That's a possibility," I said.

"Well, we can't just leave it like that," said Linda. "If she doesn't come here, we should go to see her in Fruitvale sometime."

"I think my parents would let me have the car," said Dennis, reminding us all that he is now sixteen and has a driver's license.

"But would we want to ride with you?" said Julio, teasing him.

"It's important, I think," said Linda, "that we have a chance to say good-bye if she's moving back home, and if she comes back to Collinsville, it's important for us to act as if nothing has happened."

"But it has," I said. "We were really worried about her and concerned about her, and I think she should know that."

"I think we need to tell her that we're her friends and that we wish she would have shared her feelings with us," said Kimber. "If she doesn't know how to be a friend—like Jon said—then we need to help her know how to be a friend."

34

"She probably doesn't need a lecture, though," said Linda.

"Mrs. Miller has probably already done that," I said, "although I really don't know what happened when she finally got to Fruitvale."

"Why don't we try to put ourselves in Trish's shoes?" Ford asked.

"Good idea," said Jon. "What would we want to have happen if we were Trish and we were coming back to the group after running off like that?"

"I'd want a party!" said Julio.

"Yeah," said Dennis. "I'd want people to say they missed me. No lectures. No spankings. Just a good time."

"No heavy guilt-trips," said Ford.

"Love just might be the best response," said Linda.

"It usually is," said Jon.

And then I got a great idea! "We could make a friendship bracelet for her," I said.

"A what?" asked Dennis.

"A friendship bracelet. Baker's has these beads—you know, Baker's Craft and Hobby Store—that you can put together to make bracelets and necklaces that you design. We could go as a group and make a bracelet for her, with each one of us choosing a special bead."

"That would be neat," said Linda.

"It *would* be a good show of friendship," said Kimber.

"What about you, Libby?" I asked. "Do you think you could do that?"

"Yeah," said Libby. "Don't get me w-w-wrong. Just because I'm m-m-mad, doesn't mean she isn't my f-f-friend."

"Right," said Jon.

"You mean no party?" said Julio.

"We could do a party, too," said Dennis. "But first we need to know if she's coming back or we're going there—and when."

And that, of course, became the second half of our emergency meeting last night. After we had brought everybody up to date on the Frisbee tournament, we shifted into high gear to plan Trish's party. It's going to be at Mrs. Miller's house. We're going to meet there at six o'clock to be ready and waiting when they drive back from Fruitvale. Mrs. Miller is going over to pick up Trish and she has promised she will call me tomorrow afternoon just before they leave Fruitvale so we'll know about when to expect them to pull in. Should be great! But first . . . a good night's sleep.

Decisions, decisions, decisions. It's been a big week for planning.

Chapter Three

Welcome Back!

The party was a big success! At least as far as I could tell. Trish was really surprised, that's for certain.

We all met at Baker's just as we had planned, and the more we got into designing something for Trish, the more beads we wanted to have. We ended up making a necklace instead of a bracelet, and it was really neat. Baker's has a big selection of beads—lots of different shapes, sizes, and colors, and also some unusual things that you can hang on cords or chains between the beads. We got a "T" for Trish, to hang at the center of the necklace, and we also scattered nine heart-shaped beads among the other beads, one for each one of us: Kimber, Libby, Jon, Ford, Julio, Dennis, Linda, and

37

me . . . plus one for the Lord. We figured that would be a good way to send the message that we *all* love Trish a lot.

While we were figuring out the beads, we got the idea to make FF bracelets for ourselves. So we did. We made up our own designs of beads and then included two beads that had the letter "F" on them as part of our designs. I think we just about cleaned out Baker's supply of F's!

In the afternoon, I met with Libby to make a big peach cobbler. Trish had told Libby one time that peach cobbler is her favorite dessert. Dad volunteered to make some homemade ice cream for us, so we obviously took him up on that offer! I was surprised when Libby declined an opportunity to pretaste the ice cream. She said she's trying to lose a few pounds—she's already lost five pounds this summer and wants to lose five more before I teach her how to swim. She got a neat swimsuit at Clara's and she's eager to show it off, I think. Good for Libby! It's one thing to lose weight because you want to, and another thing to lose weight because other people want you to. I asked her if she was going to have cobbler at the party and she said, "Probably not," and then quickly added, "But don't t-t-tell anybody. I don't want to make a big d-d-deal out of this."

"OK," I said. "But I think you're a really good sport to come help make this cobbler when you aren't going to have any of it. Isn't it hard to cook and not eat?"

"Sometimes," Libby said. "But then I say to myself, 'That w-w-wouldn't really look very good with my swimsuit.' When I think about things being a-a-accessories to a swimsuit, it's pretty easy to resist."

"Good idea!" I said. "I'll have to remember that if I ever need to lose a few pounds."

"You?" Libby said.

"Sure," I said. "Nearly everybody has to watch their weight at some time or other."

"But you're so thin," she said. "You'll never have a weight problem."

"I hope not," I said. "On the other hand, my mother was a few pounds overweight. She never made a big deal out of it and it certainly never bothered Dad or Kiersten or me. But I remember the day when she took off a pair of jeans that were too tight and said, 'Out of jeans, I guess, and into jeans skirts!'"

"At least she had a good sense of humor about it."

"That's one of the things I miss most about Mom," I said. "She always was able to find something to smile about in life. Kiersti is like that, too. I think it's a special gift they have."

"I wish I could have met her," said Libby.

"Me, too," I said. "But then again, if Mom

hadn't died, we wouldn't have moved to Collins-ville and I wouldn't have met you, Libby!" I leaned over to poke Libby in the ribs and she gave me a hug. "Life has a way of going on."

After the cobbler was out of the oven and cool-ing, Libby went home to change clothes and I changed, too. I don't know why, but I really wanted to look extra good last night.

Mrs. Miller had left me a key to her house, so Dad and I went over a few minutes before six so we'd be there when everybody else arrived. Dennis was smart enough to park his car around the end of the block and everybody else put their bicycles behind the house where Trish wouldn't see them when they drove in the driveway.

We had a good time putting up crepe-paper streamers, and the neat banner that the guys had made. Kimber and Dennis brought a little bicycle pump with a special adapter that Dr. Chan had found, so they were able to blow up balloons really fast. We had them all over the living room. Libby and I set the table. Julio "practiced" a lot by taking photos of what he called the "before-party party."

And right on cue, Mrs. Miller called at 6:15 to say they were just leaving and they'd be back about 7:15. That was just the right amount of time.

"Do you have the feeling we're giving a party

for the prodigal son?" said Dennis as he hung some streamers from the dining room chandelier.

"I can see why the father in that story thought a party was a good idea," I said. "When somebody you care about has been away, you're so glad to have them back that you forget all about the way they left."

"Right," added Ford. He really looked good. I could tell he had just had his hair cut and he was more dressed up than usual. When he walked past me, I even got a big whiff of after-shave! Wow. He must really have it bad for Trish! Actually, now that I think about it, it seemed as if everybody had the same idea—to try to look their best for Trish's homecoming.

At precisely 7:17, Mrs. Miller and Trish pulled into the driveway. We had pulled the curtains so she couldn't see any of the decorations through the front windows, and we had the lights off and were all hiding behind the sofa when they walked in.

You should have seen Trish's face when we all jumped up and yelled "Welcome back!" She was really shocked, but then she got a big grin on her face and said, "So much for scaring me right into paralysis." It was such a Trish thing to say.

We all gathered around to give her hugs and I couldn't help but notice that Ford gave her an extra special hug. In fact, we all got into it. Julio shouted,

"Hugs all around!" and we all started giving each other big bear hugs and then more hugs. Mrs. Miller had tears in her eyes but a big grin on her face. I think she was happy to have us all there, and happy to see Trish happy. (Jon gave me a big hug and in the process picked me up and twirled me around. I had no idea he was that strong. He really surprised me.)

None of us brought up the subject of Trish's leaving without any notice, but after we had all helped ourselves to cobbler and ice cream, she brought it up. "I'm sorry if I caused you guys to worry," she said. "Gram told me that I made some of you a little crazy. I really don't know what got into me. I guess the bike trip to Benton gave me the idea that I could ride that far, and don't laugh, but I originally intended to ride over to Fruitvale and *back* all in one day."

"Super Woman!" said Julio.

"Super Crazy Woman," said Libby.

We all laughed. Then Libby said, "You mean, you didn't really mean to l-l-leave me with all those pizzas for two whole w-w-weeks?"

"No, I didn't," said Trish. "I'm really sorry about that. And I'm sorry I lied to you, Libby. If you don't want to give me my job back at Tony's, I'll understand. You deserve to keep it if you want."

"No way," said Libby. "I'm ready for a v-v-vacation. You start on Monday!"

"We *were* really worried, Trish," said Kimber.

"Actually, some of us were pretty jealous," said Dennis. "Having never cycled fifty miles in a day . . . what was it like?"

"S-o-r-e," groaned Trish. "I could hardly move my legs the next morning."

"We made something for you, Trish," said Jon, handing her the box with the necklace from Baker's. Trish opened the box and immediately put on the necklace. "Thanks, guys," she said. "You're the greatest."

"We all love you, Trish," I said. "And we hope that necklace is a reminder so you won't forget that we really do care what happens to you." I explained to her about the hearts.

"I don't deserve you guys," said Trish. She leaned over to give me a hug and Julio again kept the moment from getting too intense by calling out, "Hugs all around!"

We told Trish all about Jon's idea for the Frisbee tournament and about the City Council meeting and about all our assignments. "What's my job?" asked Trish.

"Well, we thought you might want to help Ford make the containers that are going into the stores," I said, coming up with an assignment totally off the top of my head.

"Is that OK with you?" Trish asked Ford.

"Sure," said Ford. I could tell by the way Trish

asked her question that she doesn't have a *clue* about how Ford feels. I wonder if I should tell her? Hmmm. I'll have to think about that a little.

We didn't stay very late since we knew that Trish still needed to unpack and settle back in. She seemed to have brought over quite a bit of stuff from Fruitvale—considering that she took nothing with her when she left Collinsville.

It sure feels good to have her back. One thing I noticed, though, was that Trish got really quiet when I told her about the nine hearts and one of them being a symbol that the Lord loves her. She acted almost as if she didn't want to hear that. I think I'm going to ask Mrs. Miller if she knows how Trish feels about God. Right now, I've got to get ready to go to youth group. They announced at church this morning that we're going to get to see a special movie at group tonight. It's one I saw back in Eagle Point but I'm really excited to get to see it again. So . . . later, Journal!

Chapter Four

Catching Up

I never get tired of going to The Wonderful Life Shop. All the pretty things to look at . . . the well-worn smoothness of the countertop . . . the delicious aroma of candies and flavored coffees . . . the sound of the front-door bells, the clanging cash register and, mostly, the oohs and aahs of customers. I like everything about Aunt Beverly's store.

And it really felt good to get back after being away for two whole weeks. The first week I stayed at home because Mrs. Miller was away, and the next week Aunt Beverly suggested I take off just because I had so much to do to get ready for the City Council meeting and the FF meeting and the party. It felt good this morning to get back to an old familiar routine.

Mondays and Tuesdays are always pretty slow days at the shop. (That's one of the reasons I take off Mondays.) Tuesday is the day when Aunt Beverly and I usually spend time unpacking boxes, dusting everything thoroughly, and restocking supplies. Aunt Beverly usually does most of her ordering on those two days and while she's busy making calls and filling out forms on Tuesday, I get to wait on any customers who come in, or help her with her filing. It's amazing how much paperwork it takes to run a shop. Sometimes I feel as if we're working in an office! Occasionally, Aunt Beverly will send me on an errand—to the post office, for example. But the very best part of Tuesdays, as far as I'm concerned, is that Aunt Beverly and I get to talk more than we usually do. It's always a good day for catching up.

Now that Aunt Beverly is dating Mr. Clark Weaver pretty regularly (or at least that's the way it seems to me; Aunt Beverly still denies they are "dating" and says they are just good friends), she doesn't have dinner with us as often as she did when we first moved to Collinsville. When she does have dinner at our house, it seems there's always lots to talk about besides the shop or Aunt Beverly's life—like how things are going down at Stone's Hardware or what Kiersten did during the day, or what our schedules are like for the rest of the week. Tuesday talk is talk that is more relaxed, and from the heart.

I know it doesn't seem possible, but today was the first time I really had a chance to ask Aunt Beverly in private about her evening out with Jon and his dad—the night the three of them went to dinner almost two weeks ago!

"By the way," I said, "where did you and Jon and Mr. Clark Weaver have dinner a couple weeks ago?"

"Dinner?" asked Aunt Beverly.

"Yes, dinner," I teased. "You don't need to try to hide it. Jon told me the three of you were going out together. It was on a Wednesday, if I recall. Almost two weeks ago."

"Oh, that dinner," said Aunt Beverly. "I wasn't trying to be secretive. I really didn't remember. Two weeks is a long time for this old memory. Let's see . . . we went to The Barn."

The Barn is just what it sounds like. It's a for-honest barn—a pretty small one actually, made of stone—that has been turned into a restaurant. It's down on the south end of town, across the river. It's a nice place to eat and lots of people go there. We've only been once, with Dad and Grandpa Stone. It takes longer to get there than our favorite places downtown, and it takes a little longer to eat there, too. Sometimes there's a wait to be seated and the service isn't always real fast. But it's got

47

good food—especially their spaghetti and meatballs—and it's a good place to go with people if your main reason is to talk and not just eat.

"What did you have?"

"I tried their goulash soup. It was really pretty good. They served it with homemade bread and a hunk of white cheddar cheese. It felt like a downhome farm meal in a barn!" laughed Aunt Beverly.

"Sounds good. Jon said that he thought you had something you wanted to discuss with them. Was it about your idea for a men's shop?" I asked.

"Yes," laughed Aunt Beverly. "You really are my personal mind reader, aren't you, Katelyn?" With that, I got a big personalized Aunt Beverly specialty hug.

"Well?" I asked, a little afraid that Aunt Beverly was going to go on to other subjects.

"I haven't kept you very up to date on this, have I?" asked Aunt Beverly. "It's not that I've wanted to keep it a secret . . . I'm just not one hundred percent sure what is going to happen."

"Well, like the song goes that I like so much . . . 'start at the very beginning, it's a very good place to start,'" I said, and started to sing.

"Enough, enough!" said Aunt Beverly. "I think I heard *The Sound of Music* a hundred times that week I visited you and Kiersten in Eagle Point—remember the time your folks went on vacation and I got to be your baby-sitter? You were probably only about seven years old."

"I remember. It's the first time I really knew that you were a *fun* aunt, and not just a come-to-visit-occasionally aunt."

"Thanks," said Aunt Beverly with a grimace.

"Well, we did read the entire collection of Beatrix Potter books, remember?" I asked. "And we made Flopsy Bunnies out of felt. It was a kit you brought to us, remember?"

"I remember. I also remember that you and Kiersten wouldn't eat anything unless I put sprouts on it because you were pretending to be bunnies . . . and that you wanted to stay up late every night."

"That's what made it fun!"

"And also tiring. It's one thing to raise two little active girls from birth. I discovered it's another thing to try to keep up with them if you don't have any practice!"

"Back to the store, Aunt Beverly," I said, trying hard to keep things on track. I know that *I* have a tendency to wander around a bit when I talk or write, but I'm beginning to wonder if I got that trait from Aunt Beverly.

"Do you remember when we went over to Benton to see the fireworks on the Fourth of July?" Aunt Beverly asked.

"Sure." (Come to think of it, dear Journal, I

49

don't think I ever told you about it. I can't imagine why not. Maybe because it all seemed so *quick*. Fireworks were always a big thing at Eagle Point—with the big bursts of color popping over the water of Eagle Bay. We usually took a big picnic hamper to the beach and joined our friends there—especially the McGillans. They were a little like our adopted grandparents until Mr. McGillan died and Mrs. McGillan went to live with her daughter. Here in Collinsville, there really isn't much of a Fourth of July celebration. A few people have sparklers, but just about everybody goes over to Benton. There is a big fireworks show at the Benton Community College football stadium, and it really is pretty neat. We made it a family-only event—Grandpa Stone, Aunt Beverly, Dad, Kiersten, and me. Jon and his father went out of town that weekend and so did Kimber and her family. Libby had to work that night at Tony's—filling in for a girl named Marcia, not for Trish. Anyway . . . we just stopped at the Burger Haven in Benton for cheeseburgers and then went to the stadium. It felt strange not to be in Eagle Point. Mom always loved fireworks so it made us all a little sad, I think—as if something was missing. The evening felt more like a chore in some ways than a fun outing. Not that it was a bad experience—it was just a little melancholy. Anyway, back to the conversation I was having with Aunt Beverly. . . .)

"Do you remember my introducing you to a girl—a woman really—named Colleen? She was with a friend named Maggie?"

"Yes, vaguely."

"It was pretty quick, I admit," said Aunt Beverly.

"They were at the concession stand!" I added, suddenly remembering exactly who, where, and what.

"Right," said Aunt Beverly. "Colleen has been working in a men's department for lots of years and we met at a group called the Benton Christian Career Women's Forum a few years ago. The Forum has since disbanded—we all had schedules that were impossible—but Coll and I still meet for lunch occasionally. We seemed to have lots in common, and for a while we even talked about being roommates. She has dreamed for years of opening her own store, but just hasn't been able to save the money for it. Her friend Maggie has also worked in men's retail and is now a buyer."

"So Colleen is the one you think might manage the store?" I asked.

"Right. You're a step ahead of me. She told me last time we had lunch, which was before I saw her at the Fourth of July show, that she was thinking about moving out to Collinsville. She would like to buy a house, rather than live in an apartment in Benton. Maggie has been thinking about

51

buying in with her so they could both afford a house more easily. So . . . I talked to her about the idea of a men's store for Collinsville. And she jumped at the idea. She talked it over with Maggie and she thought it would be a great opportunity, too. But then last week, Coll said that she thought Maggie was having second thoughts—the idea of moving into a new house and a new town, and starting a new store, all seemed a bit overwhelming to her."

"Colleen can't run the store by herself? You run this shop by yourself."

"Well, not entirely. I do have *you* as a helper," said Aunt Beverly.

"Right, but I'm not always full-time."

"True. Retail clothing, though, takes a little more personal shopper attention. You know, helping someone find the right sizes, putting together different looks. It's hard to wait on more than one or two customers at a time. And if you're helping someone, the cash register goes unattended," explained Aunt Beverly.

"I get the picture. So what does all this have to do with Jon and his father?"

"One of the things that Coll and I talked about was the general look and design of the store, and the kinds of lines that she would want to carry. We both agreed that she should really go for the junior high and high school crowd—lots of classics and a few funky things. We'd like to see all the guys at Collinsville High look as neat as Jon has been looking."

"Well, you're the one who transformed Jon's look," I said.

"He had all the basics, though—not to mention a very handsome face and tall, strong physique," said Aunt Beverly with a wink.

"Yeah, he is pretty cute," I said. "The amazing thing is that he doesn't think so. A lot of guys seem so stuck on themselves, when some of them really don't have all that much going for them. And then there's Jon, who looks great and has a great personality but doesn't think he's got much."

"I think you've helped him a lot in that area, Katelyn," said Aunt Beverly, sounding a little more serious.

"All I try to do is tell him the truth," I said.

"That's what Jon needs to hear. That's really what every person needs to hear. The *truth* is that most people have a lot more assets and good points than faults, but they see themselves just the other way around."

"I still don't get the connection with the store."

"Well, one of the things that Coll and I thought would be a good idea would be to have a fashion board, and name some of the guys at Collinsville High and Collinsville Junior High to it."

"A fashion board? You mean like Brookings of

Benton?" (Brookings is a really neat dress shop up by the community college. A lot of college girls shop there. A group of really fashion-conscious girls is chosen each year to model. Aunt Beverly told me one time that the girls also help the store owners decide what to offer in the shop.)

"Right, only for guys. And we certainly wouldn't call it a fashion board."

"Smart idea," I said. "I'm not sure the guys I know could relate to that term."

"Well, we figured that guys probably couldn't relate to the entire concept of a fashion board very well, so we thought we'd probably not ask the guys to do anything—only use their photos."

"And Mr. Clark Weaver is a great photographer—"

"Exactly," said Aunt Beverly. "What Coll and I had in mind were large photos of local guys in the clothes sold by the store—pictures as big as four feet by six feet. The photographs would be the wall decorations for the shop. Black and white. That way we could change them as the seasons change.

"How many guys would you have on display?" I asked.

"We thought two per school grade, starting with seventh grade. That would give us twelve photos. What do you think?" Aunt Beverly asked.

"I think it's a super idea. But how would you decide which guys to choose?"

"Well, our idea was to have Clark come to the shop with some of the guys that work out with their dads at the Collinsville Family Fitness Center. They'd come the week before we opened. We'd also have Mr. Ray there with his scissors and blow dryer. Coll and I would put together a look for each guy and Mr. Ray would do his hair, and then Clark would take his photograph. The guys would get a free hairstyle and we thought we'd give them fifty dollars' worth of clothes of their choice to keep. What do you think?"

"Neat. I think I'd like to be a fly on the wall so I could watch."

"Well, maybe we could use a fly on the wall to help us stay organized," Aunt Beverly said.

"So . . . did Mr. Clark Weaver and Jon think this was a good idea?"

"Frankly, I was a bit surprised at their reaction," said Aunt Beverly.

"In what way?"

"Well, Clark thought the photography would work out fine, but he didn't really want to talk about the photos as much as he wanted to hear the full business plan for the store—how much money it was going to take to get it started, when it would open, what kinds of clothes we'd have, why we were limiting ourselves to teens. I was surprised that he wanted to hear so many details."

"Do you think he wants to be a partner in the store?" I asked.

"No, I don't think so. I don't think Mr. Clark Weaver is all that into fashion, do you?" Aunt Beverly giggled.

"No, I guess not," I agreed. Mr. Clark Weaver always looks great, but his wardrobe consists primarily of shorts, shirts, caps, and Birkenstock sandals. He's very much Mister Casual. "Maybe he was concerned that you'd be too busy with the store to have time for him?" I added.

"Now there's an idea," said Aunt Beverly. "But, no . . . I don't think that was it either. He just seemed very concerned whether I had thought everything through and was going about this in a very objective, rational manner. And . . ." Her voice trailed off.

"And what?" I asked.

"And I sensed a little concern that he thought I was putting a lot of money at risk."

"Are you?" I asked.

"Perhaps," said Aunt Beverly. "I don't think of it as a risk as much as an investment. But it does mean quite a bit of up-front cost—renovating the shop area, signing a lease with Miss Jones, advertising, buying the initial inventory. I'm not an expert in men's retail, either, so I have to rely quite a bit on Colleen's knowledge and instincts."

"Maybe that's what was concerning him—that you wouldn't be totally in charge."

"I don't know. It was just a little strange. I don't feel as if I really know Clark well enough to tell him about my finances. He wasn't exactly prying—it felt more like genuine concern—but at the same time . . ."

"Do you think he was trying to find out how much money you have, Aunt Beverly?" I asked.

"Could be," she said. "And maybe not."

"Well, why not just tell him that you're the most successful businesswoman in town?" I said, half joking, but also half serious. Aunt Beverly is a fabulous businesswoman from what I can tell. She has a shop that has lots of customers and makes lots of sales, a really neat house, and she pretty much does what she wants to do and buys what she wants to buy.

"In the first place, that's not true. I'm not the most successful businesswoman in town," Aunt Beverly replied.

"Who is then?" I asked.

"There are a number of women who own more property or have a higher volume of monthly income, I'm sure. Miss Jones is without a doubt the wealthiest businesswoman in this town right now, because she owns so many buildings. But money isn't what's most important to me. I like to take on challenges and see them become good realities.

I'm interested in starting this men's store to a great extent because I think Collinsville needs a men's store, I think it would be a fun challenge, I'd be learning something new about business—"

"And making some money," I interrupted.

"Precisely," said Aunt Beverly. "And I really wouldn't want Clark Weaver thinking that I was the wealthiest woman in town."

"Why not?" I asked. "Do you think he'd like you less if he thought you were?"

"You never can tell, Katelyn. Telling a man how much money you have or make can be tricky business."

"Why?" I asked. "It doesn't seem to me that it should make much difference, unless, of course, you were going broke."

"Well, some guys are intimidated by women who make a lot of money—especially if the woman makes more than he makes. Other guys are looking for a woman who makes lots of money so they can freeload off her."

"But don't some women do the same thing with guys?"

"True enough, I guess. But most women don't feel intimidated if a man makes more money than they do. That's a problem for some men."

"Do you think it would be a problem for Mr. Clark Weaver?"

"I don't know. Like I said, I don't feel as if we

know each other well enough for me to tell him everything about my finances. In fact, I have to know a guy *really* well before I want to tell him all my secrets," said Aunt Beverly with a grin.

And at that, the front door opened and in came a couple of customers. Aunt Beverly went over to greet them and to offer them a free cup of coffee while they browsed. The flavor today was Orange Cappuccino. It smells heavenly—almost good enough to make me want to start drinking coffee.

I've been thinking about what Aunt Beverly said and I can see her point. It's not money so much that matters to the kids I've known at school . . . it's *things*. Some guys seem bothered by girls who have nicer things than they do, or who live in bigger homes or whose parents have fancier cars. Other guys seem to want to be with girls only because they come from families that have a lot of money. It's a strange way for the world to work.

I've never heard Jon mention money or things one way or the other. I wonder if he thinks Aunt Beverly is rich. Or if he even cares. Does he think Grandpa Stone and Dad are rich—which would make me a "rich girl"? I hope not. That's hardly the case. We have nice things and live in a nice house, but I don't think anybody would call us rich.

When Aunt Beverly was free again, I asked her

the question I had wanted to ask all morning. "What did Jon think of the men's shop idea?"

"He thought it sounded like a great idea. He said he'd shop there, especially if I'd help him put things together," said Aunt Beverly. "He even joked a little and asked if we'd take in Grandma Turner's mistakes."

"He had on an outfit just a few days ago that he said was from Grandma Turner. I think her taste is improving," I said.

"It probably helped for Clark to have sent Jon's grandmother some photos of his new look," said Aunt Beverly.

"Is that all Jon said?" I asked.

"No . . . ," said Aunt Beverly. "He seemed very embarrassed by the idea of the photographs, and especially my suggestion that he be one of the guys featured."

"Typical Jon," I said. "He probably couldn't figure out why you'd want him to be a model."

"That was part of it, I think," said Aunt Beverly. "But he said something that has bothered me a little each time I think about it."

"What was it?"

"He said, 'I don't think I'm the kind of guy you want to have up on your wall. You need popular guys there. I'm a nobody. I'd probably scare people away—especially if they thought that buying clothes at your shop would make them turn out to be like me.'"

"What is it with him?" I said, feeling a little annoyed. "Why do you suppose he has such a poor image of himself?"

"I don't know," said Aunt Beverly. "I asked Clark about it later and he said that Jon has always been something of a loner—that the friends he's made here in Collinsville are the best and the most friends he's ever had."

"That makes me sad, Aunt Beverly," I said. "Jon has so much going for him. Who wouldn't want to be his friend?"

"Well, I seem to recall a certain girl saying not more than two or three months ago that he wasn't anybody that *she* cared to get to know," Aunt Beverly laughed.

"That was before I knew Jon," I said.

"It's hard for some people to make friends," said Aunt Beverly. "People may have judged Jon on the way he looked or excluded him from their group because he is so smart. Who knows? The point is, Jon still doesn't see himself in a completely positive light."

"I'm going to work on that," I said. And dear Journal, I *am* going to work on it. There's no reason why Jon Weaver should hide his light under a bushel. (That was a neat Sunday school lesson we had just two weeks ago. Our Sunday school teacher said that low self-esteem is one of the bushel baskets that lots of people hide under.)

After that, we seemed to have a steady stream of customers for several hours. In fact, neither one of us got to eat more than a few bites of lunch. Things didn't get quiet until about five o'clock. I just had to ask as we were tidying up the shop a bit before closing.

"You still like Mr. Clark Weaver, though, don't you, Aunt Beverly?"

"Sure," she said brightly. "Why wouldn't I?"

"Well, I thought maybe that business about the money . . ."

"Heavens, no," she said. "That's about the only uncomfortable moment I've had with Clark. He's a very easy person to be around. We've got lots of things in common, and it's really nice to spend some time with a guy who is a Christian."

"Sounds like dating to me," I said.

"Just friends," Aunt Beverly said.

"So when does 'just friends' become dating—given the fact that you go so many places together and do so much together?" I asked.

"Are you and Jon dating?" Aunt Beverly asked.

"No!" I said.

"But don't you spend a lot of time together and go places together?" she asked.

"Yes . . . but . . ."

"But what?" Aunt Beverly asked.

"Well, we've never talked about being boyfriend and girlfriend. We're just friends. We don't like each other in that way."

"Ditto," said Aunt Beverly. "It might be a little different with grownups. Let's just say there's no level of commitment between us."

"You'll let me know if you start dating?"

"Maybe," said Aunt Beverly.

"Maybe?" I teased. "Maybe your maybe's are what keep you from being committed?"

"That just might be, my insightful and brilliant niece," said Aunt Beverly with a grin and a hug. "But right now, we'd better hurry up and close this shop or I'm going to be late for my nondate dinner engagement with Mr. Clark Weaver!"

Chapter Five

One-Two-Three Talks

Thursday
9 P.M.

*S*ome weeks seem to be filled with activity. And other weeks seem to be weeks that just have a lot of conversations in them. This has been a "talk" week.

After I had a good chance to catch up with Aunt Beverly on Tuesday, I came home to have yet another talk with Mrs. Miller. She was just finishing up preparations for dinner when I got home, but Dad and Grandpa weren't in yet, and Kiersten was still over at Mari's house.

"How's Trish?" I asked. "Does she seem glad to be back?"

"I think so," said Mrs. Miller. "It's different now than before she took off for Fruitvale. She seems much more content at being here. Tony was nice enough to give her back her job at the pizza place. I think Trish said Libby was still going to be able to work there part-time, too, so Trish was glad about that."

"I think Libby wanted to work only part-time. Her little brother is in a day camp in the mornings and she's supposed to watch him in the afternoons until her mother gets home. It's better for her if she only has to work dinners and not lunches."

"It was nice of Libby to fill in for Trish."

"Mrs. Miller," I said, "something has been bothering me and I don't know what to do about it."

"What is it, dear?" said Mrs. Miller, genuinely concerned.

"It's about Trish and that's why I haven't said anything about it. I don't want to gossip about Trish or talk behind her back, but I think I need some advice."

Mrs. Miller sat down at the kitchen table with me, her cup of tea about half empty. "I'll keep what you say in confidence," she said.

"Trish always seems to get real quiet every time we have prayer at the FF Club meetings, or at youth group, or even when somebody brings up the name of Jesus or mentions God. I can't tell whether she's upset or if she's just very private in what she believes."

"I know what you mean." Mrs. Miller nodded.

"And I haven't wanted to say anything because I didn't want Trish to think I was judging her in any way. Do you have any advice for me?"

"I'm not sure what to say, Katelyn," sighed Mrs. Miller. "I'm pretty much in the same boat you're in. I suspect that Trish may be going through a real spiritual struggle right now, and I'm afraid that if I pry too much, I'll cause her to clam up all the more. I do know that this isn't the way Trish was as a little girl."

"What do you mean?"

"When Trish was a little girl—oh, maybe five or six years old—she spent an entire summer with me. That was another time when her parents were having some troubles—both in their business and in their relationship with each other. Trish was the most delightful child I'd ever been around—including my own and all the children for which I've baby-sat or kept house down through the years. She loved going to Sunday school and talking about God and saying her bedtime prayers. In fact, most of the time when I'd find her alone, I'd find her looking through Bible picture books or singing the songs she had learned at Sunday school. Trish wanted to pray about everything in those days—it didn't matter how big or small the problem was. She was bubbly and happy and had enough faith to move mountains."

"I can imagine Trish that way as a little girl. She sounds a little like Kiersti."

"Very much like Kiersten," said Mrs. Miller. "In fact, there's not a day that goes by that I don't think about Trish being like Kiersten when she was her age."

"Do you know what caused her to change?" I asked.

"No, I don't," said Mrs. Miller. "It might be partly that she's a teen-ager now and going through normal growing-up questions and changes. It might be something else."

"Do you think I should talk to her about it?" I asked, almost afraid, a little, that Mrs. Miller might say yes.

"I don't know, Katelyn," said Mrs. Miller. "I think you should do what the Lord leads you to do. Pray for Trish. And pray about whether you should talk to her. If the Lord wants you to say something, He'll give you the opportunity, and urge you to say something, and then give you the right words to say. At least, that's what I believe."

"That sounds like a good idea. I've got to admit, I haven't really prayed for Trish. Actually, I don't pray very much for any of my friends. That's probably something I should do more."

"Sounds like a good idea to me," said Mrs. Miller. "Why don't you and I agree together, Katelyn, that we'll each pray for Trish every night—for something very specific. And then have a talk like this again in a few weeks."

"It's a deal," I said, and leaned over and patted Mrs. Miller on the shoulder.

"What's a deal?" asked Kiersten as she bounced into the kitchen through the back door just in time to hear what I had said.

"It's a deal we're going to keep your Christmas gifts a secret until Christmas Day!" I said.

"Christmas?" asked Kiersten, very skeptical to say the least. "That's light years away."

"That's why it's going to be so hard to keep a secret for that long," I said, with a teasing smile.

"Is dinner a secret, too, or can I know what that is?" asked Kiersten.

"Tuna casserole à la Mrs. Miller," I said. Mrs. Miller at that point got up from the table, saying it was time for her to go home. She met Dad coming in as she was going out.

Later that night, Dad found me making a prayer list in my room. "Whatcha doing, Kat-Kat?" he asked.

"Making a list of people I think I should pray for every day. I'd like to get a little more serious about prayer, Dad, but when it comes right down to it, I'm not sure I know that much about prayer," I said.

"Don't know about prayer!" said Dad, pretending to have suffered a major blow. "All those years of bedside prayers and you didn't learn anything!"

"No, that's not what I mean," I said. "I know the Lord's Prayer and I know how to pray at bedtime, but I don't really know how to pray for someone else. At night, we just tell God what we're thankful for, and ask Him to forgive us for things we've done wrong, and ask Him to keep us safe and give us health and strength and help us through the next day. When it comes to praying for other people, I seem to get stuck in a rut: 'God bless Dad, God bless Kiersten, God bless Aunt Beverly, God bless Grandpa.'"

"And that's not enough?" Dad asked, serious this time.

"It might be, but I haven't really thought about it. Mrs. Miller and I agreed this afternoon to pray for Trish every night and she suggested we pray for very specific things. I'm not exactly sure what it is that I should pray for. 'God bless Trish' just seems a little lame."

"But isn't that what you really want for Trish? For God to bless her?" Dad asked.

"Sure."

"Then all you really need to add is some specific ways as to *how* you want God to bless Trish. God bless Trish by giving her a good night's sleep. That's very specific, I'd say."

"It sounds a little like I'm trying to tell God

what to do," I said. "Who am I, Katelyn Weber of Collinsville, to tell God what to do?"

"It's not telling God what to do as much as telling God what you'd like for Him to do," Dad said. "What are all the good things you'd like to see happen in Trish's life?"

"Well, I'd like to see her happy, and feel free to pray, and to have a boyfriend, and to stay in Collinsville, and to share with us more how she feels," I said.

"Ask God for those things," Dad said. "And then give Him permission to edit your prayer."

"Edit my prayer?" I said.

"Sure. You want to be a writer someday, and every good writer has a good editor. An editor helps fix your vocabulary, spelling, grammar, and other things like that so that you are saying exactly what you meant to say. You can ask God to edit your prayer so that it's exactly what God also wants to see happen in Trish's life. In other words, tell God what you want to see happen and then give God permission to edit your prayer so that it lines up with exactly what He wants to see happen. From my experience, those are the prayers that really get answered."

"Does God always answer your prayers?" I asked, a little surprised at myself for not having ever asked Dad a question like that before.

"He always answers, Katelyn, but not always

70

in exactly the way I had hoped. Sometimes His answer is yes, sometimes no, sometimes maybe. There are times when I don't want to hear His answer, and sometimes when I just can't seem to hear it even though I'm trying hard to listen. Even in those times, though, I believe God answers. He doesn't always give me the answer I want, but I believe He always gives me the answer that's the best for my life."

"Thanks, Dad," I said as I hugged him good night. "I think I'm going to try praying some things for my friends and see how God answers."

Just before Dad turned off the overhead light and closed the door, he peeked around the door to say to me, "I love you, Katie, and I'm proud of you, too. You're growing up to be quite a wonderful young woman."

"Thanks, Daddy." I don't think I've called my father "Daddy" in several years, but Tuesday night, it just seemed right.

And so, dear Journal, that brings me to yet another conversation. This one was with Jon.

He met me at the shop at closing on Wednesday and we went directly to the park. He had an armful of bushel baskets—all painted with bright yellow and blue and white stripes (the school colors of Collinsville High). I carried four of them and he carried five—all stacked up, each basket nested partly in another basket. We looked like two clowns at a circus trying to balance a stack of twirling plates!

Jon also had some spikes and a big mallet he had borrowed from the hardware store. He also had a big pile of wire wickets, although they looked too big for croquet wickets.

"Where did you get the wickets?" I asked.

"Your dad helped me make them a few days ago. We used some of the heavy-gauge wire at the store and I sprayed them white when I did the baskets."

"How did you get all these baskets down here by yourself?" I asked. "I can hardly carry four of these. How did you carry nine?"

"Your dad brought me this far. He had to make a quick run up to the Collinsville Club to deliver some tiki-torch lights they needed for a party tonight, so he dropped me off here with the baskets."

"You did a neat job painting them."

"Thanks. Gave me something to do during lunch hours."

When we got to the park, we started outlining the course according to the map we had already drawn up. When we got to the bottom basket, I found that Jon had brought along two Frisbees!

"Want to play a hole or two?" he asked. "It could be your only time to play for free!"

"Sure!" I said. "Do you think we should let anybody know we're going to be late for dinner?"

"No problem," Jon said. "I asked your dad if I could treat you to Mexico Pete's tonight and he said it would be fine with him. In fact, he handed me a ten-dollar bill and said, 'Dinner's on me' when I got out of his truck. I told Dad this morning that I'd probably go out to eat. That was fine with him. I think he's driving over to Benton with your aunt to look at a new hutch for the kitchen."

"Well, you've got that all organized," I said.

"It's the limit of my organizational ability," Jon teased, and added with a grin, "which is not nearly as good as my Frisbee-throwing ability."

As it turns out, we played all nine holes of the Frisbee course, and it was past eight o'clock by the time we got to Mexico Pete's.

The course was really fun to play. Jon and I realized several times that we had not accounted for what we started calling "limb hazards" or "bush hazards." They made the course all that much more difficult—"Just like sand traps or water hazards on a golf course," Jon said. All in all, it was fun—but not all that easy. I scored 63 and Jon a 59. We both agreed that with a little practice we could do a lot better. I don't think I've even thrown a Frisbee in the last year!

When we got to Mexico Pete's, Pete himself brought us our menus and said, "I'm glad to see you guys came back. I thought after what happened the last time you were here, I might have lost two of my best customers."

"No way, José," said Jon, and quickly added, "no insult intended, Pete. We've both just been real busy lately."

"We really appreciate your coming to our rescue," I added, thinking to myself that I wish he would have come to our rescue just a few minutes earlier last time. "Those guys actually followed us."

"I was afraid of that," said Pete.

"But we outsmarted them," Jon was quick to add. "No harm done."

"I heard they got picked up by the police later that night," Pete said. "I'm glad they didn't catch up with you."

"We heard sirens," I said.

"Yeah?" said Pete. "Apparently the police stopped them for driving too fast in a residential area. They probably would have been given just a warning if the police hadn't spotted some open beer cans in their car."

"Really?" I said.

"They were kept in the jail until all four sets of parents arrived. And then the judge apparently talked rather sternly to all four families about reckless driving, drinking and driving, and drinking under age. The whole nine yards. They were given probation but the judge ordered them to do forty hours of community service each."

"What's their service?" Jon asked.

"I heard it was trash pick-up," Pete said.

"That sounds appropriate," Jon said with a grin. "But I'll bet they didn't have as much fun at it as we did."

"Hey," said Pete, "I saw you guys on television after you did that ride to Benton. That was great!"

"Thanks," I said. "We had a lot of fun."

"Dinner's on me tonight," Pete added, surprising us both. "I'd like to make it up to you a little for what happened."

"Hey, no problem," Jon said. "You don't need to do that."

"Don't need to, but want to," said Pete. "Let me know when you're ready to order."

After Pete walked away, Jon said, "Well, I guess you'll just have to have dinner with me on Saturday night, since I'll still have this ten dollars your dad gave me."

"What's Saturday night?"

"The next night I'm alone in the house with nobody to eat dinner with," he said with a grin. "Your aunt is cutting into my eating time."

"How do you feel about that?" I asked.

"I feel like eating out!" Jon said, still grinning.

"No," I insisted, "not about the food. About

my aunt and your dad spending so much time together."

"I like your aunt. She's a neat lady. In fact, I like her better than anybody Dad's ever hung out with."

"Hung out with?"

"You know—spent time with," Jon explained.

"Why is it that nobody uses the word 'dating' anymore?" I asked.

"Well, *I'd* use that word to describe their relationship but Dad's funny about saying he's dating anyone. I mentioned dating one time and he came right back at me with, 'We're not dating. We're just friends who enjoy spending some time together.' So . . . ," Jon said.

"I understand perfectly," I said. "Aunt Beverly is the same way. She never says that she's dating your father. It's always 'We're friends' or 'We're just having a good time together.'"

"I wonder whose idea this was to say they *aren't* dating?" Jon asked. "Was it your Aunt Beverly's idea that Dad picked up on, or Dad's idea that your aunt is repeating?"

"I don't know. It seems to me they like each other well enough."

"Yeah. I guess when it comes right down to it, it doesn't really matter what they call it, as long as they spend time together and have a good time," Jon said. But something about the way he said

76

that made me feel a little bashful—as if maybe he wasn't talking about Aunt Beverly and Mr. Clark Weaver at all.

I quickly added, "So what are you going to have for dinner?"

We agreed on sharing a big platter of super nachos, no onions and only half the jalapeños—after all, it was nearly nine o'clock. While Pete cooked, I made a quick call to Dad to tell him where we were and what was happening. It was OK with him. He just asked me to be home by ten o'clock.

Over nachos, I asked Jon what he thought of the idea for Aunt Beverly's store.

"It sounds great," Jon said. "I'll shop there. Your aunt agreed to be my, let's see, what did she call it? Personal advisor, I think."

"Personal couture advisor," I said. "She's referred to herself as that lots of times in shopping with Kiersten and me. For a couple of years, Kiersti and I thought that meant she was going to tell us when to quit shopping. We thought she was saying 'Personal quit-here advisor'! One day Kiersten said, 'Aunt Beverly, I don't want to quit. I want to shop till I drop.' Mom and I were in stitches and Aunt Beverly didn't have a clue as to what was going on. When she found out, she laughed, too. And we both learned what 'couture' really means."

"Which is?" Jon said. "Frankly, I was too embarrassed to ask her myself!"

"'Couture' is French for 'fashion,'" I said. "'Haute couture' is 'high fashion.' As in Paris and New York City."

"See, I told you I need a language advisor," Jon laughed. He knows I love talking about words, no matter what language they're in.

"Are you going to let her use you as one of the models?" I asked.

"Was that your idea?" Jon replied.

"No, but I think it's a good idea."

"I'm not sure being a poster boy is my destiny," Jon said with a grin. "I'd like to help your aunt and I don't want to hurt her feelings, but I really can't see why she'd want to use my photograph on the wall—especially such a big photograph— except maybe that she thinks she's doing me a favor because I'm friends with you."

"That's not it at all, Jon," I said. "Aunt Beverly thinks you're very handsome and that you wear clothes really well."

Jon just dropped his head and looked up at me from under the bill of the baseball cap he was wearing.

"And I think so, too," I said. If I had stopped to think about what I was saying, I might have been too embarrassed to say that, but since I didn't have any time to think, the words just came out.

"Two against one," said Jon. "How can I refuse?"

"You could at least give it a shot—so to speak," I said, feeling very witty. "If you don't like the way the photographic shoot turns out, you can always say no. And besides, Aunt Beverly said she's going to give a fifty-dollar gift certificate and a free haircut to each guy who agrees. That's not shabby."

"No . . . but it sort of depends on your perspective," Jon said. "How much is embarrassment worth?"

"You're serious, aren't you?" I said.

"You know me—Mr. Serious," Jon said, this time with a grin.

"I mean it," I said. "Would you be embarrassed?"

"Yeah, I would be," Jon admitted, as serious as he has ever sounded to me. "I can't imagine anybody taking me seriously as a model, or as any kind of 'couture expert.'"

"Why not?" I asked, keeping the tone of the conversation serious.

"Because that's just not who I am," Jon said. "What I know about fashion, I know because your aunt has specifically told me what to wear with what. As for my appearance, Mr. Ray gave me my hair and the rest of it my parents gave me. I don't get sick when I see myself in the mirror, but I sure don't say, 'Hello there, handsome!' when I greet my face in the morning."

"That's not what it means to be a model," I said. "At least not in my opinion. Being a model is simply having your photograph taken in a good-looking outfit."

"But it sends a message to other people, Katelyn," said Jon. "It sends a message that you think you *deserve* to have your photograph taken because you're somebody worth looking at, and in the case of your aunt's store, somebody other people should be copying. I just don't think I'm the guy other people should copy, and I certainly don't think I'm somebody everybody should look at and envy."

"I do," I said.

"And I'm glad you do," said Jon. "But probably not for the reason you think. I'm glad you think I'm special because I want you to be my friend and like me. I also think that you see me with rose-colored glasses, sometimes."

"Well, somebody has to," I said, teasing him just a little.

"How about this?" said Jon. "Let's agree that you can think I'm great and I'll agree to let you think that if you'll agree that I know it really isn't so but because I think you're great, I'll let you think that I'm great."

"What kind of gobbledygook language is that?" I said, laughing.

"It's what you get when you order and eat a

whole platter of nachos at Mexico Pete's this late," said Jon.

"OK," I said. "I'll agree. You don't have to be a model for my sake—not in the least. But I still think you're worthy of being a model. And you can still think you aren't—just don't try to *convince* me of it."

"OK," Jon said, looking a little puzzled. "I think."

"I think that it's nice that we've been able to enjoy an entire meal at Mexico Pete's without unwanted interruptions," I said.

"Yeah, I agree. I'm not sure, though, that we've seen the last of the fearsome foursome," Jon said.

"What do you mean?"

"I just don't think those are the kind of guys who give up easily. They haven't had their full revenge yet," Jon said.

"What do you think they'll do?" I asked.

"I don't know," Jon said. "I just hope they leave you out of it."

"That's nice of you to say, but I rather think my insults just might have contributed to their anger."

"Not that they didn't deserve what you said," Jon replied, and then added, "I wish I could like those guys or see something good in them . . . but I just can't. I've never hated anybody in my life, but those guys just might get my vote for 'least likely to make it into my like book.'"

"There's nothing that says you have to like everybody."

"Maybe not. But there is something—as in Someone—who says you shouldn't hate anybody. I've really got to fight that urge with these guys."

"Have you ever thought about praying for them?"

"About them, yes. For them, no," Jon said, and then added, "Why? Are you praying for them?"

"No," I said, "but I've been thinking lately about what it means to pray for other people and how to pray for them. I think I'm learning something, or am going to learn something, about what it means to pray for a friend. I'm not at all sure I know how to pray for an enemy."

"Well, I don't have any clues on that one," Jon said. "If you come up with something, let me know."

"OK," I said.

"You know something, Katelyn Weber?" Jon said, leaning over the empty platter between us.

"What?" I said, leaning over the same way he had. Our foreheads were almost touching.

"I think you're the only girl I've ever known who I can play Frisbees with, eat nachos with, and talk about modeling and prayer with . . . all in the same evening."

"Me, too. in reverse," I said. "We must be friends."

"I'll agree to that."

"But we're not dating, Jon Weaver," I added. He knew exactly what I meant. And dear Journal, that's the *best* thing about Jon Weaver. He always seems to know what I mean, even if it isn't what I say. I *am* glad we're friends.

Chapter Six

The Raid

CORNERSTONE BRETHREN CHURCH
AND MINISTRIES

Sunday
9 P.M.

*W*e've been raided!"

Jon's voice sounded a little higher pitched than usual, and I could tell immediately that he was *very* upset. It's not like Jon to get upset—at least not so that it shows quite so much in his voice.

"What do you mean?" I asked, trying to stay calm.

"All the Frisbee baskets in the park have been yanked up by their pegs. The police found six of them squashed, as if they had been trampled, and two of the others were up in a tree, as if they had been thrown as hard as they could be and got caught by limbs on the way down. Nobody knows where the ninth one is."

"How did you find all of this out? What happened?"

"I got a call from the police about six-thirty this morning. One of the patrol officers found that the big sign at the beginning point of the course had been spray-painted with red paint—the one that Kimber and Dennis painted and your dad and grandpa helped put in Friday afternoon. The policeman who called said he had seen our picture and the article in *The Collinsville Press* on Friday, and he also works out at the gym with my dad, so he called me."

"And . . ."

"And they asked me if they could come by and pick me up and then go to the park to see how extensive the damage was."

"So you went to the park this morning?" I asked.

"I just got back," said Jon. "They came a few minutes before seven and we were there about forty-five minutes or so."

"Who would do such a thing, Jon? All our work . . ." It had taken a while for what Jon was saying to sink in.

"Well, I have my suspicions . . ."

"Oh, no. Really? Do you *really* think The Four Creeps would do this?"

"I can't think who else would do it. We both know that lots of people had started talking about the tournament and seemed in favor of the idea."

That's for sure," I added. "When we rode our

bikes by the park yesterday afternoon, there were lots of families out throwing Frisbees, and a few couples and groups of friends, too. The park had more people in it than I've seen all summer."

"So, we know it isn't anybody *normal* who has done this—"

"And anybody who was just passing through town wouldn't know what the baskets were for, except if they'd read the sign. It's beyond me to think why a stranger would want to destroy a Frisbee course."

"No . . . it's got to be somebody who did this just to be mean, or to try to get even," concluded Jon, his mind obviously made up that Dirk, Jim, Paul, and Skip were the culprits.

"Do you think maybe it was a dog?" I asked, still not wanting to believe somebody would destroy the course just to be mean.

"You're grasping at straws," Jon said matter-of-factly. "Dogs don't throw bushel baskets up into trees, Katelyn."

"Good point," I conceded. "What did the police say?"

"I didn't tell them who I thought had done it," said Jon. "They asked me, though. I just shrugged off their question and asked if they had found any evidence. That's when we decided to walk over the course together."

"And did you find anything?" I asked.

"Well, that's when we realized that all the baskets had been taken. The police did take note of a few footprints. The best they could conclude, however, was that there was more than one person involved. They figure it's vandalism."

"What can they do about it?"

"That's the same question they asked me."

"You?" I said. "Do they think you should do something about it?"

"No, they said they didn't know what they could do to stop it from happening again, and they asked me what I thought we should do—rebuild the course and continue with the tournament idea, knowing that we might get hit again, or try some other approach," Jon explained.

"And what did you say?" I asked, eager to hear Jon's idea.

"I told them we'd have to do some thinking first, and maybe have a meeting of the FF Club."

"We can't meet today, Jon," I said. "It's Sunday."

"I know," said Jon. "But maybe we could meet on Monday?"

"I'll call everybody. This afternoon I'm supposed to go to the Collinsville Club with Libby and Mari. I'll tell Libby about the meeting then. She's already told me she won't be at church this morning. Her family has a special brunch planned in Benton with some friends of her mother's."

"Would it help you out if I called Ford and Linda?"

"That would be great! We'll probably see Kimber and Dennis and maybe Trish at church."

"And if Trish isn't at church," Jon added, "I could ask Ford to call her this afternoon."

"Sneaky," I said.

"But a good idea," Jon said. I could almost feel his grin over the phone.

"I'll see you at church."

Getting ready for church was something I definitely did by rote. I don't even remember putting the hot rollers in my hair, or taking them out. Suddenly Dad was calling us down to breakfast and I was ready. It was a very strange feeling. All I could think was, *What do we do now?*

I told Dad over breakfast what had happened and about Jon's call. He seemed a little upset but didn't say much. I don't think he wanted me to think he was upset. He did say something, though, about *possibly* calling Dr. Chan and Mr. Clark Weaver. Surely with all of us thinking together about this, we can come up with something!

I tried hard to concentrate on the songs and the sermon at church, but I must admit, I didn't have a lot of success. One thing the pastor said, though, hit home. I think he was talking about a verse in James—something about asking God for wisdom and God giving it to us liberally, which he said meant "generously." A generous dose of wisdom is just what we need right now! I should look up that passage and read it for myself.

Needless to say, Kimber and Dennis were very upset. After all, it was their sign! They agreed we needed to meet on Monday afternoon, and Kimber suggested we meet at her house. Trish wasn't at church, so Ford will get to make a call after all.

Libby was also upset when I told her about the raid as we were changing into our suits in the dressing room of the Collinsville Club. I had to be careful in what I said since Mari was there, and I didn't want Mari to get upset or think something dangerous and bad was going on. Libby just kept saying, "Justice needs to be done!" (Funny—she didn't stutter at all when she said that!)

This is the second time I've been to the pool with Mari and Libby, acting as something of a "swimming coach" for both of them. Mari has had a few lessons, but is still pretty fearful of putting her head under water. Libby had a few lessons years ago, but isn't at all confident of herself in deep water. So . . . I'm trying to help both of them feel more at home in the pool. I took lifesaving courses and even the Red Cross water safety instruction course when I was in Eagle Point—it's pretty much a given that if you are going to live along Eagle Bay, you'd better know how to swim and swim well. I couldn't get my water safety instruction license, though, because I was too young. Maybe next year. Still, I learned the information so it's fun to try out some of what I learned in helping Mari and Libby.

One thing Libby doesn't have to worry about in the confidence department is the way she now looks in a swimsuit. I was stunned. Libby always wears such loose-fitting clothes that I hadn't realized she was serious about that diet, and she really has lost weight. She says she's only lost seven pounds, but I think it looks more like fifteen! She's a knock-out in her suit—I think Aunt Beverly would probably use the word "curvaceous." That's the word she used to use in describing Mom's figure. For a while, Kiersten and I thought it meant that Mom had some kind of disease because Aunt Beverly nearly always used that word after Mom would bemoan the fact that she'd gained a pound or two. Anyway . . .

When Libby emerged from the dressing room at the Collinsville Club, more than a few heads turned.

"You look fantastic!" I said. "Too bad we have to get in the water."

"R-r-right," said Libby, obviously embarrassed by the attention she was getting. "I might look g-g-good on land, but now they're going to want to see me s-s-swim. Not good!"

"You'll do fine," I said, trying to encourage her and coax Mari into the pool at the same time.

It was at that precise moment that Julio showed up at the edge of the pool. "Hey, ladies!" he said, and I could tell he was about to shift into his fake Indian accent, which came out sounding more like Cockney English. "Methinks you are lookin' very good—a real tribute to the good taste of the Collinsville Club! You shouldn't be bothering to get into the water, though."

"Oh, Julio, you're such a charmer," I teased back. "We're here to do some *serious* swimming, though."

Julio watched a beach ball fly over his head and head for the lawn area. He got up to retrieve it for the swimmers who had hit it out of bounds. Libby whispered as he left, "Don't tell him I can't swim very well, OK?"

"OK," I whispered back.

When Julio returned he asked, "Is Kimber here? Or are you two baby-sitting Mari?"

"No—on both accounts," I said. "Libby and I are helping Mari learn a new stroke."

"Maybe I can help," Julio offered. "I've got a job here now, did you know?"

"What are you doing?" I asked.

"I'm an assistant swim teacher," he said, flashing us a big proud smile, "and a part-time lifeguard!"

"Why didn't you tell us before?" I said.

"I just got the job last week. I'm taking over some of Tad's hours. He's getting ready to leave for college in three weeks, and he's got lots of things to do."

"Great!" I said. Libby nodded and smiled, too. She didn't look very positive about the idea of Julio helping with Mari's instruction. Julio, however, jumped into the pool, ready to join us.

"How can you lifeguard and t-t-teach at the same time?" Libby asked, flashing me an "I can't believe he's doing this and what are we going to do now" look.

"I'm not on duty for another hour," Julio explained. Turning to Mari, he added, "Why don't you show me what you can do?"

Mari was eager to show off and immediately began to swim toward the other side, kicking madly and holding her arms out in front of her, but refusing to put her face in the water. The result, of course, was that her back stayed curved and she didn't go anywhere fast, and she looked more like a person drowning than a person swimming.

"Hey," said Julio. "Not bad. But always remember, Mari—just being average isn't good enough. You've got real potential to become a *good* swimmer. Let me show you a few tricks."

And with that, Julio was off and running with a first-rate swimming lesson. I was really impressed.

He didn't put down Mari at all. And she really tried extra hard to show him what she could do. He had us playing ring-around-the-rosy together so that Mari would put her head under water, and then he began playing underwater games with her. Mari had seemed reluctant to do those same games with me, but I guess Julio's being a "big guy" was impressive. Then he showed her how to hold on to the edge of the pool and blow bubbles as she kicked. Libby and I did the same thing, supposedly to encourage Mari. Little did Julio know that Libby was gaining confidence even as she was supposedly helping to teach.

Finally, Mari was ready to take off toward the other side of the pool again. And this time—she really took off! Back straight, legs splashing, arms held out . . . she was really moving. Unfortunately, she started moving in the wrong direction, straight past Libby toward the deep end of the pool. Without thinking, Libby took off after her. Julio didn't think anything of it, and I was the furthest away from them both. By the time I realized what was happening, Libby had caught up with Mari, who was clinging to her tightly, suddenly quite frightened to find herself in deep water and unable to touch the bottom of the pool. Libby was going under fast and trying to get free of Mari so she could struggle to get some air for herself.

"Julio!" I said. "Libby needs help!" He went into

93

action right away. I climbed out of the pool and raced over to get the net that's used for skimming leaves off the pool. I held it out to Libby so she could grab hold of it just as Julio reached Mari, dove under her, and then pushed her up so her head was above water, which meant she quit struggling. Within seconds, Julio had pushed her to the edge of the pool. She grabbed hold of the edge just as he came roaring up out of the water to catch his own breath. I leaned down to talk to Libby, who was coughing and choking, but was all right. It was a tense couple of moments. The lifeguard by this time had come rushing over to our side of the pool, aware that Libby and Mari had been in a little trouble, but also aware that Julio and I were in gear.

When we all got out of the pool and collapsed into the lounge chairs next to it, Julio sighed, "Let's not all try to swim at the same time, OK?" That sent us into giggles, and I don't know which was worse—laughing until we couldn't catch our breath, or nearly drowning. Actually, nearly drowning was far worse, but it was probably a good thing we didn't dwell on that fact.

"Something happened to my radar," said Mari, when she finally caught her breath.

"Yeah," agreed Julio. "You were headed for the south seas of China there, kiddo."

"That's why I need to keep my head up," argued

Mari, appearing to take one giant leap backward in her swimming progress.

"No way," said Julio. "We just need to get you going with arm strokes so you can get your bearings. Maybe even learn the breaststroke so you can see where you are each time you make a full stroke."

Mari seemed agreeable to that idea, although not particularly enthusiastic.

"And I probably need lifesaving c-c-class," said Libby.

"You did the right thing," said Julio. "You just didn't get under Mari before she climbed on top of your head. It's an easy mistake to make when you do in-water rescues."

Julio sounded so professional, I thought surely Libby would just let the matter slide or change the conversation. Instead, she said, "The fact is, Julio, that I don't do very well in deep water."

"What do you mean?" Julio asked.

Libby took a deep breath and said with a big sigh, "The fact is, I'm not that great a swimmer and Katelyn has been helping me as well as Mari."

"Really?" said Julio, but he sounded genuinely interested, not surprised or shocked.

"Really," said Libby, and then added, "I'm just a land-lubber, I guess."

"Do you know how to tread water?" asked Julio.

"No," said Libby. I felt like a dunce when she said that. It never dawned on me that Libby couldn't tread water or keep herself afloat. No wonder she was upset every time she got into deep water. I had thought it was a fear of the water. Instead, it was just that she didn't know what to *do* in deep water!

"Well, that's the trouble," said Julio. "Once you know how to tread, you've got deep water licked. I can show you if you want. In fact, I'll bet you could learn in ten minutes or less."

"Ten minutes or less?" asked Libby. "Are you sure?"

"Katelyn can time us," said Julio, sounding very confident.

"If you really think it's that easy, I'm willing to risk drowning again," said Libby.

"I won't let you drown," said Julio. And something about the way Julio said that sounded a little unusual to me. He sounded—well—tender. Gentle. Kind.

Mari was not at all reluctant to get back into the pool. I was glad about that. In fact, she didn't seem to realize how dangerous the moment had been when she was in a panic and on top of Libby in the deep water. So . . . with Mari eager to get back into the pool and try the technique Julio had taught her, I got back in with her and let Julio and Libby go off by themselves.

Mari was like a mad woman, eager to swim back and forth, back and forth across the pool. Now that she could really *move* in the water, she was eager to see how far and how fast. I knew Kiersten was going to get an earful of success story as soon as Mari got back home.

Every once in a while, I'd glance over to the deep end, and sure enough, there Libby and Julio were, bobbing up and down in the deep end—and eventually Libby was gracefully treading water (with a big smile on her face, I might add).

By the time four o'clock came—which was the time we had agreed to meet Dad at the entrance—Libby and Mari were both tired but very pleased with themselves. They both had made a lot of progress in one afternoon, without much help from me, I must admit. If it hadn't been for Julio, things wouldn't have gone nearly so well.

"Julio was right," I said to Libby as we were changing clothes. "It did take only about ten minutes for you to get the hang of treading water. I'm sorry I didn't think about that before, Libby. Some teacher I am."

"You're a g-g-great teacher, Katelyn," Libby said, and I could tell she was sincere. "Actually I'm glad I got the chance to know Julio a little b-b-better."

"He's a really nice guy," I said, trying to sound casual.

"I think so, too," said Libby. "A lot of guys

would have made fun of me for not knowing how to handle deep water, or for doing the wrong thing in trying to help Mari. He just took it all in s-s-stride."

"From where I was standing, you two seemed to be having a pretty good time down at the deep end of the pool," I said, teasing her a little.

"You were probably standing too far away to get the whole picture," said Libby, but she was smiling nonetheless. "Julio was very nice to me, that's all."

"Oh," I said, but obviously not convinced.

"Well, almost," added Libby.

"What do you mean, 'almost'?" I asked. "He wasn't one hundred percent nice?"

"No. He *was* one hundred percent n-n-nice, but that wasn't all," said Libby. "You're getting me confused, Katelyn."

"Sorry," I said. "What more did he do?"

"Well, he asked me if I'd like to come to the pool on Wednesday as his special guest, so that he could teach me how to dive."

"He did?" I asked.

"Yes," said Libby, with just a hint of smile.

"And?" I said. "You're going to take him up on that, right?"

"I think I just might," said Libby. "I told him I'd have to check my schedule at Tony's first. But I'm pretty sure I can get someone to work for me

98

that day. I'll let him know at the FF Club meeting tomorrow night."

"This is sounding a lot like a date," I said.

"Just friends," said Libby.

"Oh, sure, just friends," I said, teasing her all the more. "That's what they all say."

"Well, that's what *you* say all the time about Jon," Libby said. She had me there.

"But it's true," I said. "Jon and I *are* just friends."

"Are you sure?" Libby asked.

"Yes!"

"Is that what Jon thinks, too?"

"Yes!" I said. "In fact, we talked about it just the other night at Mexico Pete's. We agreed that we're glad we're *friends*."

"Friends . . . or *just* friends?" asked Libby.

"Look, there's Dad," I said, glad that Dad had pulled up at just that moment. I really didn't want to continue that conversation. Mari was eager to tell Dad all about her swimming the width of the pool with her face under water, and Libby told about treading water, and we were at Libby's house before any more could be said about Jon or Julio.

Libby and Julio? It's an interesting possibility, dear Journal. One thing I did notice, and which I just might point out to Libby, is that she didn't stutter at *all* when she was talking to Julio. That seems like a good sign to me!

Libby and Julio. Kimber and Dennis. Ford and

Trish—possibly. Is the FF Club going to turn into a couples club? Jon and Linda and I are the only ones who don't seem to be pairing up. What if Jon started liking Linda? I'd be the odd man out! I don't like *that* idea at all. Maybe it's time to expand our membership a little.

I'll think about it later. Right now, I've got some serious thinking to do about The Four Creeps and about our ripped-up tournament course at the park.

P.S. By the way, dear Journal, I looked up that verse in the Bible. It's James 1:5 and it says, "If any of you lacks wisdom, let him ask of God, who gives to all liberally and without reproach, and it will be given to him."

Chapter Seven

The Plan

$\mathcal{I}$ was glad Monday was my day off from The Wonderful Life Shop. It gave me more time to think through some things related to our problem at the park, and to make a few phone calls.

The faces of Dirk, Jim, Paul, and Skip haunted me off and on all Sunday night. Or at least it seemed that way. I don't think I actually dreamed about them. But I did wake up several times in the night, and each time I could hardly get back to sleep because I started thinking about them.

I don't think I've ever described these guys for you, dear Journal. Now might be a good time.

In the first place, they're all going to be seniors this year. I guess that's part of the reason they're so cocky. None of them is very good in school, or at least that's Jon's opinion based on their performance in his computer class. Dirk, I think, is the most intelligent one of the four. He's also the ringleader, or so it seems. What he says, the others do.

Dirk is about two inches shorter than Jon and Ford. He's a little taller than Dennis—about Julio's height. He's average in build with sandy-colored hair and lots of freckles. He always seems to wear his T-shirts and pants extra tight. That must be part of his tough-guy look.

Paul is the driver. He's the one always behind the wheel of the old blue and white Pontiac they cruise around in. He also comes across as the meanest one of the bunch—everything he says has a sneer to it. He's got dark hair, kind of slicked back. And he always wears a loose vest over his T-shirt.

Skip is pretty short and very wiry looking. He's got brown hair and is the best looking of the four guys. He knows it, too. He walks like he's just been named king.

Jim is a bit of an oaf—big and lumbering. He doesn't look at all bright. He's got thin brown hair. It's really easy to imagine him bald and with a big pot belly when he's middle-aged.

None of these guys is particularly strong or powerful acting when he is by himself. But when you put the four of them together, it seems they form a "force field" that can really be intimidating.

Dad says there's always a reason for people to act the way they do. I'm sure it must be true for these guys. It's hard for me to figure out, though, what could have made them want to be so mean to other people. They aren't particularly poor. They all live in pretty nice neighborhoods. I think Julio said that Jim's parents are divorced and he lives with his mother, but as far as I know, the other guys all come from homes with both a mom and a dad.

One thing I'm pretty sure about is that they aren't Christians. I don't see how anybody could be a Christian and do what they do.

Then again, I'm still not one hundred percent convinced that they are the ones who tore up the course at the park. There's really no evidence to prove they did it, and I'd like to think that people are still innocent until proven guilty in our country. Jon, on the other hand, is so convinced that these guys are responsible, he's a bit unreasonable.

We had a major argument about that on Sunday night after youth group. Jon wasn't able to go to youth group so he called me after I got home to see what had happened, and we got into a big discussion about The Four Creeps and the damage to the course. Jon thinks I'm being naive for wanting to give them the benefit of the doubt. I think he's being judgmental. Unfortunately—or perhaps fortunately, depending on your point of view—

we're both strong-willed enough to tell each other exactly what we think. It's one of those cases where we are probably both right, to a degree, but as of tonight, neither one of us is eager to give much ground to the other. I wouldn't say we're fighting. We're just not agreeing.

Even though I wasn't working yesterday, I went down to the shop in hopes that I might have lunch with Aunt Beverly. It worked out just as I had hoped. We went to McGreggor's for tuna salad sandwiches and chocolate sodas. I told her what had happened Saturday night, but she already knew about it. Both Dad and Mr. Clark Weaver had called her. As it turns out, Dad and Mr. Clark Weaver had talked together, and so had Dad and Dr. Chan. I was relieved to know that they are concerned as much as we are. All in all, Aunt Beverly said the adults agreed to support us in whatever we decided to do as a club. (It's really nice, dear Journal, to know that you've got a backup team!)

Aunt Beverly suggested that I call both *The Collinsville Press* and the mayor's office to let them know what had happened over the weekend, and to say also that we'd have a decision about what we are going to do after our meeting on Tuesday. I asked her if she thought I should also call KCOL, the local radio station, and she said she thought that would be a good idea. So I did! The editor of *The Collinsville Press* was very nice. He asked if Jon and I would be willing to come down for a second interview and story on Tuesday during our lunch hours. The man at KCOL also asked us to call and give him an update about what we intended to do.

I had a nice talk with the mayor himself! I was surprised at that. I called his office, thinking that I'd only be able to talk to his secretary, but she put me right through to him. He sounded concerned about the vandalism in the park and said that he'd talk to the police chief about it and see what more might be done to make the course secure. He also said that he hoped we'd decide to continue with our plans to have the tournament.

I called Dad after I talked to the mayor and he suggested I come down to the hardware store and talk to both him and Grandpa, which I did. Jon joined us in a "meeting" of sorts in Dad's office.

Grandpa Stone offered to replace the bushel baskets free of charge if we decided to redo the course, and Dad also suggested a way we might anchor the baskets into the ground so that they'd be more secure. It would take a little extra effort but it would be worth it. I wish we'd asked Dad in the first place how to anchor the baskets. Basically, we'd have to dig about a six- to eight-inch hole in which to set each basket. And then rather than drive the pegs straight down in the ground like we did the first time, we'd drive three or four stakes through the sides of the baskets about two inches from the bottom of the basket and into the ground that's around the basket—a little like spokes radiating from a central hub of a wheel. Dad's engineering background really showed itself!

Dad and Grandpa Stone also told us that they hoped we wouldn't decide to try to take revenge against anybody—that they'd rather see us outsmart the vandals than beat them up. Jon and I both agreed that was the best way to go. Jon did say, though, that he thought a way should be found to make the vandals pay for the damage they'd caused—quickly adding, "assuming that we can find out for certain who did this." (For Jon, that was a major concession—one that didn't go unnoticed by me!)

On Monday morning, I called Trish to make sure that she knew about the meeting. (Sure enough, Ford had called.) She said that she and Ford had talked about what had happened and they thought that we should offer a reward for any information that might lead to the identification of the kids who had caused the damage. It was funny hearing her talk about "those little punks." She and Ford apparently think the vandals are junior-high kids who need some stronger parental discipline.

When we met at Kimber's house at seven

o'clock, all of these ideas and conversations were shared by everybody involved. Our main concern, though, was to make some decisions and see what we could do to turn a bad situation into something good.

Within just a few minutes, we had all agreed that we wanted to go ahead with the tournament. No letting the bad guys get us down!

Kimber and Dennis said they'd repaint the sign on Friday morning, and Jon said he'd be happy to replace the baskets. Ford and Julio volunteered to help him paint the baskets and dig the holes to put them in. Trish also volunteered to help, which obviously brightened Ford's evening!

"The real problem," said Libby, "is not in reb-b-building the course, but in making sure this doesn't happen again."

"That's right," said Julio. "We need to come up with a security plan."

"Do you really think whoever did this will try to destroy the course again?" I asked. "Wouldn't that be kind of risky?"

"I think these guys thrive on risk," said Jon. "Destroying the course a second time would just make them feel all the more powerful."

"I agree with Jon," said Dennis. "Whoever did this can't be all that bright. They'll probably try the same stunt again."

"Will they be able to pull up the baskets,

though?" asked Kimber. "It sounds to me as if the baskets are going to be a lot more secure now."

"They will be," said Jon, "but somebody could still stomp them or damage them, or pull out the spikes with a little effort. It depends on how much they want to trash the course."

"Couldn't we ask the police to patrol the park?" Libby asked.

"I think the mayor pretty much promised that they would patrol it more," I said. "But they can't stay in the park around the clock."

"And we can't be there 'round the clock, either," said Trish. "We all need our beauty rest," she added, fluffing her hair and batting her eyelashes.

"No," said Julio, "but we might be there when they are!"

"How are you going to figure out when that is?" Kimber asked.

"Well, maybe we need to start thinking like the crooks," said Julio. "When is the prime time they are likely to strike again?"

"I don't have a clue," I said. "How can you know that?"

"Well, I think you can narrow it down," said Julio. "They'll probably try to trash the course either a few days after it's rebuilt . . . or just a few days before the tournament. I'd say three or four days either way."

"If there's an article in the paper that says we're

going to rebuild," said Ford, "then they'll know exactly when the course will be rebuilt."

"You mean, if we rebuild the course on Friday and there's an article in the paper that same day, you think they'll try to damage it Friday night, Saturday night, or Sunday night?" Jon asked.

"Right," said Julio.

"You don't think that they would assume that's the time when everybody is going to be on high alert?" asked Dennis.

"I don't think they're smart enough to think that through," said Jon. "I think these guys are totally motivated by hate. They aren't trying to make a name for themselves. They're just trying to make sure that something good doesn't happen."

"You make it sound like you think they've set themselves up to be our enemies," said Trish. "Do you have an idea who these guys are?"

"Well," began Jon, glancing in my direction. I know I had a scowl on my face. Jon concluded simply, "I have my suspicions."

"You think it's the guys who tried to run you down out on Highway Nine when we were doing our litter patrol, don't you?" asked Trish.

"I think it could be," said Jon.

"Then this is a matter of revenge for them," said Julio.

"They might not even care if they get caught," added Dennis.

"Oh, I don't think they want to get caught," said Jon. "I think they just don't want us to succeed with this tournament."

"So we're back to where we s-s-started," said Libby. "What can we do?"

"I have an idea," said Linda. "We could hide in the park and catch them the next time they come to do their little monkey business. It wouldn't be such a big deal to have a stakeout for two or three nights. We'd probably only need to stay out there until midnight or so."

"Our parents might even join us," said Kimber. "I know my father is pretty upset that somebody has done this. He's really concerned that a gang might get started in Collinsville."

"I know my dad will help, too," said Jon.

"I think several parents would help," I said. "But what exactly are we planning to do if we catch these guys? Call the police?"

"Sure," said Linda. "Why not?"

"I think that would only make them all the madder," said Jon. "The police aren't going to do much. After all, they're still minors and this is not exactly the same as robbing Fort Knox. They'd probably just get a slap on the wrist, and the next time they might try something even crazier. I'd hate to see anybody get hurt by these guys."

"That's right," said Ford. "We don't want a war with these creeps. We just want to trip them up—like in that old movie *The Sting*."

"Never saw it," said Libby.

"Well, these guys . . . aaw, it's too complicated. I'll just rent the video for you someday."

"OK," said Libby. "Maybe we can have a party."

"I say we shoot 'em," said Julio very seriously. Now *that* got everybody's attention! All eyes turned to Julio and there were a few seconds of silence.

"You're not serious," said Trish.

"Yeah, I am," said Julio. "I think we should shoot 'em." Everybody seemed frozen, until Julio added with just the faintest of smiles, "With our cameras."

"Whew," said Libby, "for a minute there I was getting worried you might be t-t-turning into a major bad hombre."

"You might have something there," said Jon. "What's your idea?"

"Well, we hide like Linda said. And we each have cameras. If we see them, we take their picture."

"And then?" I asked.

"We let them know we have them on film and if they ever try anything like this again, we'll turn them in."

"That just might work," said Jon.

"Wouldn't it be a little dangerous?" asked Kimber. "What if these guys have some kind of weapon?"

"Well, in the first place, we'd outnumber them—probably three to one by the time we got a few parents involved," said Julio. "In the second place, I don't think these guys tote guns or knives. I've never seen them do anything but threaten people with clenched fists or shoving and name calling."

"We'd have to be sure to stay together," Libby said.

"Yeah, and make sure we got good pictures," said Jon. "My dad could probably teach us how to set our cameras so we'd get the best exposures."

"Good idea," I said, and was glad to see Jon smile at me. I've missed his grin the last couple of days.

"Speaking of parents," I said, "I think we should talk this over with our parents."

"Right," said Libby. "I can just see me asking my dad, 'Can I go out and play with my friends in the p-p-park until midnight?'"

"They need to know," said Kimber. "And they might also have some more ideas for us."

"How about a meeting on Wednesday with our parents?" I asked.

Everybody agreed that sounded like a good idea. So we left it at that.

In the meantime, Jon and I went to *The Collinsville Press* for an interview at noon. The editor said he was going to do a front-page follow-up, and he took some pictures of Jon and me with three of the smashed baskets. (I was glad Jon had brought the baskets along.)

We also called KCOL on Tuesday afternoon and we did an interview with them over the phone. It was fun! Jon and I got on the two phones in our house so we could have something of a "conference call" with the reporter at the radio station.

I called the mayor's office. The mayor was out but his secretary told me that she'd give him the message. She sounded happy that we've decided to rebuild the course and go ahead with the tournament.

Aunt Beverly, Dad, and Grandpa Stone have all agreed to go to the meeting tomorrow night at the Chans. Libby called just a few minutes before I started writing tonight to say that her dad had agreed to come to the meeting. She was really excited that he was coming. It's the first time her father has shown any interest in the FF Club.

Jon also called tonight to say that his dad is going to bring his camera to the meeting tomorrow night. All in all, it feels as if a plan is coming together.

I hope we catch whoever has done this. It would be terrible to have the course destroyed a second time. Now that we've come up with a stakeout plan, I'm kind of looking forward to this weekend. It feels like an adventure.

Even Kiersten is excited about it. At first she thought she was going to get to go to the park with us, and she was a little disappointed when Dad said she couldn't go. Then he said later that he had made a couple of calls and Kiersten and Mari would probably spend the evenings together with Mrs. Miller as their baby-sitter, either at the Chan house or at our house. That changed everything! Having a friend sleep over two or three nights in a row sounded like even *more* fun to Kiersti!

She can be so cute at times. Just a little while before I came up to my room, she walked in with an old "detective kit" she got for Christmas a couple of years ago. She gave it to me with an announcement that there still seemed to be plenty of ink for making fingerprints, and even some chemicals for getting fingerprints off the baskets. Actually, that's not all that bad an idea.

In some ways, I can't believe we're actually doing this. In other ways, I can hardly wait until Friday night!

Chapter Eight

All Systems Go!

*T*he plans are all set. Tomorrow we put the course back into shape. And tomorrow night we start our stakeout.

We had a great meeting with our parents last night. Ford's dad came with Ford and Linda, and Libby's father came with her. Mrs. Miller was there. So were both Dr. and Mrs. Chan, and both of Dennis's parents. Julio's dad came. And Mr. Clark Weaver. Aunt Beverly. Dad. Grandpa Stone. And two of the guys that work at Stone's Hardware who just wanted to help. With all of us, and not counting Mrs. Miller (who is going to baby-sit for Kiersten and Mari), we have a stakeout team of twenty people! That's pretty amazing.

I'm feeling a lot better. There seems to be more

safety in numbers, and this way, if it *is* The Four Creeps, we've got them outnumbered five to one!

We divided ourselves up into teams of two for Friday night. Each team will have one large flashlight and one camera. Jon brought the map we made of the park and we decided who was going to be where. We're going to meet at our house at 9:30 on Friday evening and walk to the park, everybody dressed in dark clothing. It all seems to be pretty organized.

Jon's dad gave us a brief lesson in nighttime photography, and told us what speed film to buy and how to set our cameras. We're going to have to use a lot of wisdom in taking photos. Those of us who have flash cameras need to make sure that the culprits are within ten to twelve feet of us. Otherwise, the flash won't pick them up and we'll just have dark photos. Or we can try to use a tripod and a time exposure. That's a lot trickier, and not as good if there's lots of commotion. It's a wait-and-see proposition.

Between now and then, we each have to make sure we have film and enough batteries in our cameras (and our flashlights too), and have flash attachments or bulbs for our cameras. Jon and Julio are also going to have video cameras. They'll be using pretty bright floodlights. Jon is taking hole number one. Julio is taking hole number nine, also near the parking lot. We figured that those were the first two holes the vandals would probably try to hit.

Each team has a particular hole on the Frisbee course to watch. And then two adults are watching the parking lot.

Oh, yes! We're also taking whistles with us. Whoever spots the vandals first is supposed to take a photograph and then blow the whistle as loudly as possible. Then we'll all converge on the hole where the vandalism is occurring. If there are two holes hit at the same time, we're supposed to go to the one closest to us.

My partner for Friday night is Trish. That should be fun. Especially if we can keep from giggling. We're guarding hole number four. Trish is going to man the camera and I'm going to have the flashlight and whistle. This is starting to get exciting!

Today at The Wonderful Life Shop, several people mentioned to me that they had seen the article in the paper and thought the tournament was a great idea. They hadn't tried to play the course, though, and they hadn't heard about the damage. Three of the people put money in the cannister next to the cash register. Aunt Beverly said she had seen several other people put money into the cannister earlier, so I decided today might be a good day to make my rounds and empty all of them.

Trish and Ford did a great job making the cannisters. They got somebody to cut up an old rusty pipe for them and they splattered each piece of pipe with a little bit of paint. The pipe looks like some of the pieces of playground equipment that are made with a similar style of pipe. They also made a sign for each piece of pipe that reads, "Help fix up the equipment in our park!" They put "Sponsored by the FF Club" in small letters at the bottom. They made a bottom for the pipe out of tight-fitting cardboard, but left the top open for people to drop in coins or dollar bills (we hope, we hope).

At the end of the day, I emptied the pipe into our cash bag and we had more than twenty dollars in the pipe at The Wonderful Life Shop. Grandpa Stone brought home the money in the container at Stone's Hardware, and that was twenty-three dollars. He said people all day had been talking about the tournament and the need to fix up the park benches and equipment. I ran by McGreggor's, Tony's, and Mexico Pete's, and there was a little money in each of those containers, too. In all, we've already collected nearly fifty dollars!

I didn't get to Clara's, Baker's, or the River Gorge Café, but I'll try to get there before the weekend is up.

Having that much money means that tomorrow morning I can pay Grandpa Stone for the bushel baskets, and also pay Kimber back for the materials she and Dennis used to make the sign. With the money from the mayor, we're going to buy some wire brushes so we can start scraping off some of the old chipped paint from the benches and swing set. Grandpa Stone said we need to do that before we can paint.

Kimber and I thought we'd start in on the scraping while Dennis, Jon, and Julio were digging the holes for the baskets and reinstalling the course. We even thought we might talk the guys into a pizza afterward. (Trish said she had permission from Tony to give us a discount if we came by on Friday.)

It's going to be a busy weekend!

Oh, yes! Another thing . . .

Trish came into the shop this afternoon to get a birthday present for her mother. She needed to get something that would be pretty easy to mail— I guessed from what she said that she isn't going to be able to go over to Fruitvale for her mother's birthday. It sounded as if her mother might be out of town, visiting an old friend.

Aunt Beverly helped Trish find just the right thing—some beautiful notecards that look like they are made out of lace. I think she said that the cardmakers use a laser to cut out the designs. They are really beautiful. And to go along with the cards, Trish picked out some lacy sachets in old rose and pale pink. It will be easy for her to send all of that in a padded "book bag" mailer. A really nice gift.

While Trish was in the shop, we had a chance to talk a little about Friday night. Aunt Beverly suggested we might want to take a break and go down to McGreggor's for a soda. That sounded like a great idea to me! I could hardly believe my ears when I heard that Trish had never been to McGreggor's for a soda. Anyway, we didn't have any customers in the store, so it seemed fine to take a little break. I really haven't had much of a chance to talk to Trish alone since she got back.

I asked her about making the containers with Ford.

"We had a great time," Trish said. "He's a cool dude."

"I think so," I said, eager to hear more.

"He's got the most incredible computer system I've ever seen. All kinds of scanners and other things he can plug into his system. And without a doubt, more games than I've ever seen in one place other than an arcade."

"Maybe we should ask him to give us all a tour sometime."

"I think he'd like that," said Trish. "He seems pretty shy, but once you get to know him, there's a lot to Ford. The pipes were his idea, you know."

"No, I didn't know. But I think they look great.

And they're obviously working. People are putting money in them," I said.

"I hope so," said Trish. "Ford and I went over to the park to check things out on Sunday afternoon, and some of that play equipment really is in pretty bad shape."

"So that's where you were. We missed you at youth group."

"Actually, I went to youth group with Ford—at his church. They've got a good group of kids, although I think I like Faith Community Fellowship better, all things considered. It was fun, though. They had something they called 'Bible Bowl.'"

"Bible Bowl?" I asked. "Like Super Bowl?"

"A little, yeah," said Trish. "It's a game. I think they must have divided everybody up into two teams quite a while ago. Since I was a visitor, I just joined Ford on his team. The leader of the youth group asks questions about the Bible and then the person who knows the answer wins points for his team. They're keeping a running score, and right now, Ford's team is ahead by about twenty points."

"That's a pretty good lead," I said.

"Not really," said Trish. "I think the score is three-sixty-five to three-eighty-five, so it's a pretty tight match."

121

"Wow, you're right," I said. "How many points do you get for a right answer?"

"Five," said Trish. "So you can see, they must have been at this a while. They asked twenty-five questions on Sunday night, and I think that's how many they ask each week. Ford said the competition has been going on for several weeks."

"Did Ford score any points?"

"He got three right answers," said Trish. "What was even more amazing was that *I* got a right answer!"

"All right!" I said. "What was it?"

"How many of each species of *clean* animal did Noah take into the ark?" said Trish.

"What's the answer?" I asked.

"Seven," she said. "Everybody always thinks that the animals went into the ark two by two, but mostly it was seven by seven. Gram taught me that years ago."

"Did you go to Sunday school when you were a little girl?"

"Yeah," said Trish. "It was a little tiny church. We didn't live in Fruitvale then, but in a place called McArthurville. I think they changed the name a few years ago to something else. Anyway, it was about an hour beyond Fruitvale—a really little town."

"A wide place in the road?" I asked.

"You got it," said Trish. "It had only one

church—I think they called it a community church, but it had a Sunday school for all the kids—everybody, no matter your age, was in the same class."

"Did you like it?" I asked, curious but not wanting to sound too curious.

"Yeah, I did," said Trish. "God seemed a lot simpler then."

"What do you mean?"

"You know, things were a lot more black and white. It wasn't so hard as a little kid to figure out good and bad."

"I know what you mean," I said. "It was easier when Mom and Dad just *told* us what was right and wrong."

"It can be confusing to figure all that out now," said Trish, "at least to me. Take for instance my riding off to Fruitvale. At the time, it seemed like a good thing to do. Once I got there and realized how upset Gram was, it seemed like a really bad thing. Seeing my parents, though, seemed like a good thing. And at first I thought *they* thought it was a good thing. Except when they found out what I had done—riding my bike and all, and not telling Gram first—then it seemed like a major bad thing. Now . . . well, now I don't know whether it was bad or good. I'm glad I went . . . sort of. And I'd do it again . . . I think. But I'm sorry for making everybody crazy . . . a little at least."

"Good example," I said. "We went through some of those same feelings. When you first rode off, we all thought it was a bad thing, but then when we started thinking about how you must be feeling and about your being with your parents, it sort of started to seem like a good thing."

"The best thing, though, was coming back," said Trish. "It really meant a lot to have you guys all there when I got back."

"We were eager to see you!" I said.

"Yeah?" said Trish, with a little question in her voice. "Nobody was that glad in Fruitvale. The kids there that I had thought were my friends just took the attitude, 'Oh, *you're* back in town.' It's almost as if some of the girls were jealous or something."

"They might have been, Trish. You'd be major competition to any girl who wanted to compete with you for something."

"Me? Who would think I was competition?"

"Why wouldn't you be?" I asked. "You're cute and have a great personality and you really know how to communicate with people and you're fun to be with. If you and another girl were after the same guy or ran for the same office in school, I think they'd see you as nearly unbeatable competition."

124

"But none of you take that attitude," Trish said.

"Are your friends in Fruitvale Christians?" I asked.

"I don't know," said Trish. "I never thought about it. I'm not sure that makes any difference."

"I think it might," I said. "Christians, at least in my experience, don't compete with each other quite as much."

"I don't know about that," Trish responded. "I know some people who call themselves Christians who can hardly wait to put other people down."

"Maybe they aren't real Christians."

"I guess that's another one of those maybe-so, maybe-not areas for me," said Trish. "Not everybody is good who claims to be. Probably those we call bad aren't as bad as we think they might be. I'm a hundred percent convinced that not everybody who calls himself a Christian is the kind of person I'd trust with my back turned."

"What really matters is how a person feels about God, don't you think?" I asked, feeling as if this conversation had somehow become way too deep for sodas at McGreggor's.

"I guess," said Trish. "But frankly, I run hot and cold on that one, too. You're going to think I'm awful, probably, but since we're being real straight with each other . . . there are times I'm not too sure how I feel about God."

"What do you mean?" I asked, almost afraid to hear her answer.

"Well, sometimes I wonder if God even cares. Does it matter to Him that my folks are having a really hard time staying married? Does it matter to Him how I feel about watching them argue and then not speak to each other for weeks? Does it matter to Him that I rode my bike to Fruitvale by myself without telling anybody? Does it matter to Him that I'm living with my Gram instead of my folks, in a new town? I don't know if any or all of those things matter to God or not. And if some of them matter and some of them don't, which are which? Most of the time lately, I think that probably not very much that we do matters to Him. If it does, He certainly doesn't let us know."

"Like what?" I said. I had a feeling that Trish was about to lose me in this conversation.

"Like kids getting hurt or wars going on. Why doesn't God do something about that? A lot of innocent people are in big trouble."

"Maybe God expects *us* to do something," I said. Aunt Beverly and I had a conversation like this about a year ago and I still remember what she said. I had asked her the same thing after seeing a TV program on crack babies. Aunt Beverly had said, "Well, Katie, I think sometimes we look up to heaven and say to God, 'How can you let that happen?' and I think God looks right back at us and says, 'Good question. How *can* you let that happen?'"

"You're saying that you think God expects us to do something about those things?" Trish asked.

"Yes," I said. "What we do is a matter of our own wills. As a whole, what we let other people do is a matter of our wills, too."

"But there's nothing I can do to help my parents," said Trish. "I've prayed for them. I've talked to both of them. Actually, I've yelled at both of them. They just don't seem to listen, or to care, about what I say, about what other people say, about what Gram says—not even what the Bible says. If there's nothing I can do, then maybe there's nothing God can do either. Is that what you're saying?"

"No," I said, trying to figure out on the spur of the moment exactly what it was that I *was* trying to say. Trish was as good at detours as Aunt Beverly and I! "I think what I mean is this. God expects us to do some things and to fix some of the things that are wrong. And then there are other things that only God can fix. And in the case of your parents, Trish, I think that some of the things are probably things only your parents can fix."

"Well, they certainly don't seem to care what I think. They aren't at all willing to let me in on the fixing."

"Then I think you probably just have to trust

God to take care of you, no matter what they decide."

"And you think God cares what happens to me?"

"Yes, Trish, I do."

"But why? What makes you think He cares?" she asked. She had a belligerent edge to her voice.

"Well," I said, scrambling for the right words and ideas, "I guess because He's caused us to care. It's like God has put a little piece of His care for you in each one of our hearts. I know He's done that in me."

Trish's eyes filled suddenly with tears.

"And I don't understand that at *all*," she said.

"You don't believe that we care?" I asked.

"No—I know you care. I just don't understand *why* you all care," she said.

"I think it's because God put us together as friends to help each other through the hard parts of life," I said. I have no idea, dear Journal, where that came from, but it sounded really right when I said it. Trish just nodded. And we both finished slurping up the last of our sodas.

"I've got to get to Tony's or I'm going to be late," Trish said, looking frantically at her watch and brushing a tear from her cheek all at the same time. "I'll see you tomorrow night."

"Right," I said. "I've got to get back to Aunt Beverly's. We've been gone nearly an hour!"

128

We both took off in opposite directions. I made it back to the shop just as a bus pulled up! It's the first busload of people we've had all week. It seems that the tourist people are stopping through Collinsville more and more. The people always seem to pour into Aunt Beverly's shop first, and then they wander down the street to McGreggor's. A couple of the antique stores are also popular with them. Anyway, I made it into the store just ahead of the first customers and Aunt Beverly had a huge look of relief on her face when she saw me. "I was about to panic in a major way," she whispered on her way to the door to hold it open for a couple of elderly women who seemed to be struggling with the door latch.

We sold lots and lots between three and four o'clock! It was a good feeling, but tiring. I could tell Aunt Beverly was pleased. The summer is usually a pretty slow time for business—at least that's what Grandpa Stone has said—but this summer seems to be a record-breaker as far as The Wonderful Life Shop is concerned.

Dad and Kiersten and I went to The Barn for dinner. I think Dad's been wanting to go there ever since he heard that Aunt Beverly and Mr. Clark Weaver had gone there with Jon. Speaking of which, Jon and I are supposed to have dinner on Saturday night. I wonder if he's still counting on that. I think I'll give him a call. . . .

Chapter Nine

The Stakeout

*W*hat an exciting two days these have been!

Aunt Beverly let me leave the shop early on Friday—we had a steady stream of customers all morning but nothing overwhelming, and by two o'clock things were slower so she thought she could handle everything by herself. At least that's what she thought at the time. As it turns out, Mr. Clark Weaver came into the shop about 2:30 and shortly after his arrival, a busload of tourists came in. That started things humming and Aunt Beverly actually put Mr. Clark Weaver to work. She told me that night that he was a pretty good employee—in fact, the older ladies loved buying things from him!

Not knowing any of that, of course, I felt entirely free to meet Kimber at the park with wire brushes in hand. We spent two hours scraping paint from benches and the swing set in preparation for our first round of painting on Saturday morning. Meanwhile, the guys dug the shallow holes for the Frisbee baskets, which were all freshly painted, a solid bright yellow this time. We helped them with the last two holes—hard work! But by five o'clock the course looked as if it had never been destroyed (except, of course, for the change in color of the baskets). Kimber and Dennis had redone the sign in the morning. We felt as if we were back in business. And sure enough, just as we were finishing, a bunch of kids showed up to start tossing Frisbees! That was an encouraging sign. We figured as long as people are in the park throwing Frisbees, no vandalism will happen.

After we finished, we talked the guys into a pizza at Tony's, and on the way, we stopped to pick up a couple of copies of *The Collinsville Press*. They really did a nice story—they even put the offer of a reward in a little box on the front page, along with a big picture of Jon and me holding smashed baskets. The article played up the need for park equipment and made the FF Club sound like a really good group (which we, of course, know it is!). We were all very excited at what Trish later called "good ink."

On the way home from pizza—about seven

o'clock, I guess—Jon asked me if I'd pose for a couple of photographs. He said he wanted to empty his camera of film so he could reload for the night. Since there was still enough light, we went back to my house and I changed really fast into a sundress and brushed out my hair and Jon took six or eight pictures of me standing on the front porch. It was fun to pose, and he was really a cut-up, pretending to be a high-fashion photographer. It will be fun to see what turns out. Kimber, of course, is thoroughly convinced that he just wanted pictures of me—she thought the bit about emptying the camera of film was a pretty lame excuse. I don't know. It's not like Jon to make up a story. If he had wanted pictures of me, he probably would have just asked. At least that's what I think.

Right at 9:30, everybody showed up. It looked like an army converging on our street—everybody dressed in black. I stuffed my hair up under a black baseball cap I borrowed from Trish. Dennis had brought some charcoal so we could smudge our faces. That seemed like a bit much, but we all got into the fun of it and by the time we were ready to leave for the park, it would have been difficult to tell if we were good guys or bad guys. Most of all it was hard to keep from giggling.

Trish and I found a good low limb on a tree next to the fourth-hole basket and settled in. We were real quiet for the first few minutes—I think we were expecting something to happen at any second. But after a while, we relaxed and started talking in very quiet voices. Trish told me that she had called Ford on Thursday night to tell him the good news about the amount of money we had collected so far, and she also told him about our conversation at McGreggor's.

"What did he say?" I asked.

"He agreed with you," Trish said. "Katelyn, he's a really nice guy."

"I know," I said. "I'm glad you're finally figuring that out. I think he's really got a big crush on you."

"Yeah, I'm starting to figure that out, too," she sighed. "The feeling's mutual, I think."

"Really?" I said. It's hard to be excited and quiet at the same time, especially when you're sitting up in a tree trying to scope out crooks!

"I think so. He really makes Tad pale by comparison, and I thought Tad was about the neatest guy I'd ever laid eyes on," Trish said. "The thing about Ford is that he's so quiet he just kind of sneaks up on you, and then whammo, you realize that he's someone very wonderful."

"Does he know that you like him, too?" I asked.

"Well, I didn't come right out and say so, but he pretty much told me that he cares a lot about me," Trish said.

"He did?" I was a little surprised that he'd be so bold. "What *exactly* did he say?"

"We were talking about friends and caring—like we were at McGreggor's, remember?—and he just said, 'Well, *I* care, Trish. I care a lot. And I think God does, too.'"

"Now, there's an upfront guy," I said. And thought to myself one giant *YES!*

Trish said, "I think that's one of the things I like best about Ford. He doesn't seem like a guy who plays games. I've got to be really careful, because sometimes I *do* play games, and I don't want to hurt him or make him think something I really don't mean."

"You won't," I said. "It's easier to be yourself with somebody like Ford."

"You can really be yourself with Jon, can't you?" Trish asked.

"Sure," I said. "We talk over lots of stuff and Jon's always very straight with me. But that's a little different, Trish. Jon and I are just friends."

"Oh, Katelyn," Trish said, sounding just a wee bit exasperated with me, "when are you going to face the music? The guy's crazy about you, and I think you're crazy about him. You might be honest and straight with each other about lots of things, but I don't think you're being honest with each other about how you feel."

I didn't know what to say. Why is it that everybody has such a hard time dealing with the fact that Jon and I are just friends?

Trish didn't mind my silence. She just went right on, "Here I am trying to admit to myself that maybe, just maybe, God cares about me. The least you can do is admit that Jon cares about you!"

"Oh, I know he cares," I said. "I think Jon cares a lot about me. I just don't think it's a boyfriend-girlfriend kind of thing."

At that, we both heard a rustle in the bushes and saw a couple of large shadows come bounding out of the bushes straight for Frisbee hole number four! Trish leaped out of the tree and ran a few steps and then stopped and started snapping photos. I blew my whistle and then flipped on the flashlight. I should have done it the other way around—flashlight first and whistle second. Trish and I had captured two big frisky dogs! Both of which seemed delighted to see us and started barking madly as they joined in all the commotion. Of course, people came running from all directions. Which would have been really embarrassing if it hadn't been for the fact that we all had one giant laugh out of it.

"Good dress rehearsal," said Mr. Clark Weaver. "At least we know our system works!"

In going back to their various posts, Aunt Beverly and Mr. Clark Weaver (who managed to be a team . . . I wonder why!) were spotted by a police patrol car. They told the police our plan and although the police weren't particularly enthusiastic about the idea—I think they'd just as soon catch the vandals by themselves—they didn't object. In fact, they told us something that we didn't know. The park is officially "closed" at eleven o'clock . . . but they gave us permission to stay until midnight.

Which we did, and as you might have guessed by now, nothing happened. The two big dogs were the only creatures in the park besides us! Still, we weren't all that discouraged. We had pretty much given ourselves three nights of stakeout before reappraising our approach.

On Saturday morning, we all met to begin painting, which didn't take all that long. We only wanted to do a portion of the swing set and three benches to show "work in progress." We also wire-brushed the rest of the park equipment: the merry-go-round, slide, teeter-totter, monkey bars, and jungle gym. It would be nice if the park could get some new equipment. By comparison to some parks, this equipment is really old-fashioned. Still, it's fun. I don't mind admitting that after we had scraped away some of the old rusty paint, we all had a good time playing on the equipment! Especially the merry-go-round.

I just can't get over how good Libby looks. This was the first time I've seen her in something that wasn't particularly loose-fitting. She had on a T-shirt and jeans culottes, and they really showed off her new-found figure. I couldn't help but notice, also, that Julio seemed to be wherever Libby was. It's just amazing—she really *doesn't* stutter when he's around.

Mari and Kiersten came with us to the park, and it was fun to watch them try out the Frisbee course. They were a riot. Mari isn't very coordinated, so her Frisbee tended to go in every direction imaginable. Kiersten is so overly enthusiastic she was forever overshooting the mark. They had fun, though. So did lots of other people. It was a good day for the project, I think. People saw us working on the equipment while they were trying out the course. Several of them stopped to talk to us about the FF Club (we were wearing our T-shirts). A few people waved encouragement to us and said, "Good job." We saw a number of people slow down as they drove by, checking things out. I'm beginning to think this could be a very successful tournament after all!

Saturday night Jon and I did go out to dinner—to Tony's with Kimber and Dennis—and then we all met just as we did on Friday night. It was pretty much the same routine. Trish and I were so concerned about getting it right and not sounding a false alarm, I'm not sure we would have known what to do if someone had actually shown up at hole number four. As it turns out, we didn't need to worry. The vandals hit holes one and nine!

It happened just a few minutes after eleven o'clock. Suddenly we heard whistles and saw the floodlights that both Jon and Julio were using with their video cameras. Trish and I both scrambled out of our tree and by the time we got to the scene, everybody else was there, completely surrounding the culprits, who had tried to make their way back to their car. Wouldn't you know, they had on ski masks—but it was plain to see who they were anyway. Jon was right. It was The Four Creeps.

And boy, were they frantic! One of them—I think it must have been Dirk—tried to break through the ranks, but Dad and Dr. Chan caught him and put him back into the circle we had created. Trish and Libby were both shooting away like mad with their cameras, and Dennis and Ford grabbed two of the masks and pulled them off the faces of Skip and Paul. Dirk and Jim then took off their masks too, trying to get guys to fight them. Skip and Paul were both held in hammerlocks by Phil and Bobby, the two guys from Stone's Hardware.

Grandpa Stone kept saying, "Calm down, boys. We just want to talk to you."

Since it didn't look as if they had any other choice, the four guys finally did calm down.

It was at that point that Dr. Chan took over.

"Now, boys," he said. "We want you to understand the situation clearly. We've got you caught—

red-handed. There's no doubt that forensics would find your fingerprints on that basket, and be able to match your footprints with your shoes." (Jon had emptied a watering-can's worth of water around the first hole to create a little soft earth so footprints would show up. Smart!)

"So what are you going to do?" said Dirk, trying to sound tough but actually sounding a little scared. "Call the cops on us?"

"Nope," said Dr. Chan. "We're not going to call the police tonight."

"Then what's the big deal?" said Jim, stooping over to pick up his ski mask.

"We're going to get our film developed," said Dr. Chan. "And we're going to use our little kit to dust the basket for fingerprints. We're going to take some more photographs of the footprints you've made. And then . . . if anything happens to this course before the tournament is held on Labor Day, we're going to take our evidence to the police."

"But what if somebody messes up your course and it's not us?" demanded Dirk.

"Well, that's your problem," said Dr. Chan. "We suggest you boys make sure that doesn't happen."

Brilliant. It was just brilliant! Instead of being Frisbee-course vandals, Dr. Chan had put The Four Creeps in charge of Frisbee-course security! What a move! I looked over and saw that Jon could hardly keep from grinning, even though he was trying hard to look serious.

"Now get out of here," said Dr. Chan. Aunt Beverly and Libby stepped aside to let the guys move between them and walk toward their car. They roared off into the night, but we knew that this had been our victory! As soon as they were gone, we all let out war whoops and started hugging each other and jumping up and down. Even the adults seemed excited.

"How about ice cream at our house?" Dad said. I had wondered why he had filled the freezer yesterday with so many half-gallons of ice cream.

So . . . we all trooped back to our house and dished up the ice cream and talked about what had happened—pretty much everybody talking at once.

"Did you see the look on those guys' faces?"

"What a team!"

"What a plan!"

"It was just like in the movies!"

When we settled down a little, Jon and Grandpa Stone (who were partners at hole one), and Julio and Bobby (partners at hole nine) told what had happened. They had heard the old Pontiac pull into the park, but apparently without the headlights on. And then they heard the guys running toward the holes, splitting up so that Dirk and Skip went to hole one and Jim and Paul to hole nine. Both Jon and Julio waited until after they had run by their stakeout positions so that they were between the Creeps and their car. Then, almost simultaneously, they blew the whistles and turned on the cameras. Meanwhile Aunt Beverly and Mr. Clark Weaver, who were on stakeout in the parking lot, had run behind the boys and were there to stop them from getting back to their car. Mr. Clark Weaver was clicking away madly with his camera. Rather than run toward the lights and cameras, the guys tried to run the other way and circle around the lights—and of course that meant they ran smack into Dennis and Linda, and Ford and Kimber, who had their flashlights aimed on the guys and their cameras popping. The rest of us running from the top end of the park made escape impossible.

"We couldn't have done better if we'd planned it," said Julio. And that caused all of us to cheer for ourselves once again.

After lots of hugs all around, we dispersed into the night. Libby said as she went out the door, "I think this is the most fun my dad has had in years!" That was probably true for several of the parents.

We were all exhausted at church this morning, but pretty pleased with ourselves. And the sermon couldn't have been more perfect if Pastor Richardson—he's the new assistant pastor—had planned it! He spoke on Romans 8:28, which is one of my favorite verses in the Bible: "And we know that all things work together for good to those who love God."

I was surprised to see Trish at Faith Community Fellowship this morning—and Ford and Linda were with her. She said to me after the service, "He decided to come with me this week. It felt like we all ought to be together." Sure enough, all nine of us in the FF Club were there. It felt good. Big tears were rolling down Trish's cheeks during the sermon. I can tell her heart is softening. God is really doing a work. I feel like praying for her just about nonstop—my main prayer is that she'll finally come to that point of accepting God's love in her life.

Chapter Ten

The Painting Crew

*J*can't believe an entire week has gone by. It's not that I've forgotten you, dear Journal. Rather, the days have all been pretty much the same and I guess nothing seems quite as exciting as what happened last weekend.

On Monday, Libby and I spent the entire day painting at the park. We got a lot done. On Tuesday afternoon, Trish and I went around to the various places where we had cannisters and we emptied them. It was amazing. There was more than ninety dollars in what Trish appropriately called "the pipeline."

The article in *The Collinsville Press* and the interview on KCOL really moved a lot of people, or so it seems. People have mentioned the article to several of us—some of Trish's customers at Tony's, some of the people who come into Stone's Hardware and see Jon there, several of the guys who work out at the Collinsville Family Fitness Center. The whole town seems to have rallied behind the tournament—not just for fixing up the park equipment, but for showing that the town is against crime and vandalism. In addition to the money in the cannisters, there were several notes. One of them was obviously written by a child. It said, "Thank you for fixing up my park. I'm sorry you got robbed." Trish and I laughed when we read it, but in a way, that little kid had it exactly right— we felt as if we *had* been robbed.

With this amount of money, we can just about pay back the city for the paint and brushes (which we bought with the money they advanced us).

More painting on Wednesday after work. This time Jon and Ford were able to come and help . . . Kimber, too. It's fun to watch everybody's "style" when it comes to painting. I tend to be a little messy—getting paint on myself and my clothes (at least I've been smart enough to wear old grubbies). Kimber, on the other hand, doesn't get paint anywhere except where it's supposed to go. I guess that's the artist in her, or at least lots of experience with paint. Jon likes to do the impossible parts— the top bar of the swing set, for example. And Ford goes crazy if he finds "drips" or obvious paintbrush marks in what he's painted. He's the real perfectionist in the crowd. When it comes to speed, however, nobody can paint as fast as Libby. She really gets with the program.

Five of us gathered to paint on Thursday while Trish and I made a "money run" again. This time we took in fifty dollars—that should just about pay for all the paint we need, and we haven't even had the tournament yet. We probably only need to raise about twenty dollars more.

We took Friday off. Right after work, Aunt Beverly, Kiersten, and I went to Benton. We picked up hamburgers to eat in the car on the way over, so we could maximize our shopping time—all the way to the ten o'clock closing of the mall. And boy—did we ever get a lot done! Shoes. Several cute new outfits for both Kiersti and me. It was the back-to-school blitz. There's an outfit in the window of Clara's that I still want to try on, but all in all, I feel pretty set for the start of the new year. For the first day of school, I have a cute skirt-and-top outfit.

Kiersten was pretty excited about her new things. Plus, a few days ago she found a couple of things in the hand-me-down trunk that she liked, and which Aunt Beverly thought she could update with some new trim. Kiersten is taller for her age than I was, so some of my things need to be lengthened for her. She doesn't like everything in the hand-me-down trunk, mind you, and a few things she has absolutely refused to wear, but for the most part, I think she gets a kick out of having even *more* clothes because she gets some of my old things.

On Saturday, we all met and painted for an hour or so. And then we realized that we were nearly done with the equipment and we'd better leave ourselves a little work for next weekend. We don't want to get *completely* done, or people might stop giving. The problem was, there we were, all dressed for paint, our brushes ready, and plenty of paint—and nothing to paint!

"Isn't there something else we can p-p-paint while we're in the mood?" Libby asked.

And then the idea hit me. It was a real bolt out of the blue—some of my best ideas are like that! I said, "You know, I've noticed that the picket fence in front of Mrs. Miller's house needs painting. We've got plenty of white paint left. Why don't we go do that?"

Trish said, "Gram mentioned just this last week that the fence needed paint. I was hoping to do it myself . . . you guys don't need to do it."

"But we want to," said Kimber. "Besides, wouldn't that be a good way of surprising your gram?"

"Sure," said Trish. "She'd love it."

"It would be like a thank you, too, for her introducing us to you," said Ford as he put his arm around Trish's shoulder.

"Well, if you really want to," said Trish.

And so off we went, paintbrushes and cans in hand, singing the "Hi-ho, hi-ho, it's off to work we go" song from *Snow White*. (Kiersten and I still love watching that movie—it's one of our all-time favorites.)

Libby, Julio, and Dennis manned the wire brushes, and somehow they just managed to stay ahead of the rest of us who were madly painting away, trying hard not to get paint splattered on the sidewalk or Mrs. Miller's bushes. When we got there, Trish went in the house to tell Mrs. Miller what was going on, but she wasn't home. She had left a note for Trish telling her that she had gone to Benton to pick up something she had ordered from the Sears catalog. So . . . we had this great goal in mind that we'd get the entire fence done before she returned. We felt like we were racing against the clock. And we *almost* made it. We had five pickets still to go when she pulled in. I wish we had had our cameras to catch the look on *her* face. It was classic "happy surprise."

We probably would have finished in time if a puppy from next door hadn't come over to snoop around. He wanted to be everywhere our brushes were, and it was all we could do to keep his nose out of the paint cans and his tail from wagging up against the freshly painted pickets.

Mrs. Miller brought out a big pitcher of lemonade and a plate of cookies while we were putting the final touches on the fence and cleaning up our brushes. We all sat on her porch and steps admiring our handiwork, and taking turns holding that very squirmy puppy.

And that's when Trish started crying. I don't know what happened. She just suddenly put her head down on her knees and wrapped her arms around her legs and began to cry. Ford leaned over and rubbed her back a little and asked her what was wrong.

"You guys are just too much," she said. "I've never had friends like you."

"We feel the same way about you, Trish," said Jon. That made her cry all the more. I leaned over toward Jon—I was really proud of him for saying that—and he put his arm around my shoulder. It felt comfortable for him to do that.

"I've told Katelyn and Ford that I've been really mad at God lately for all the things that seemed to have gone wrong in my life this spring and summer. But you guys are something that's really gone right. I think maybe God does care about what happens to me."

"I know He does!" said Julio, and Kimber piped in at the same time, "He really does, Trish."

"I think I'll try to get things right with God this Sunday," she said, wiping her eyes.

"Why wait till then?" Jon asked. "You could do it right now—I got things right with God in my life sitting on somebody's front porch."

Trish looked up at Jon and he gave her a big grin and a little shrug of his shoulders. "Do you think?" she said.

"Sure," said Ford. "There's nothing better than praying with friends."

"OK," said Trish. And she closed her eyes and started to pray—we all gathered around and closed our eyes and linked arms or touched her. It was really neat. She said, "God, I've been really mad at You and I'm sorry I've been so mad. Please forgive me. I know You love me. And I love You, too." At that point she really started to cry. Kimber started singing really softly that old song we used to sing in Sunday school as kids, "Jesus Loves Me." Several of us joined in. And then everybody started singing. We got louder and louder and before we knew it, we were singing at the top of our lungs and laughing and giving hugs all around. Mrs. Miller had huge tears in her eyes and I could tell that the handkerchief she was clutching in her hand was soaking wet.

What a neat experience that was, dear Journal. In fact, I think it's one of the best things that's ever happened in my entire life! I get chills every time I think of it. It was just wonderful. Ford leaned over and gave Trish a sweet kiss on the forehead while we were singing and she started smiling. Actually, I think she was glowing. And that's the way I feel, too.

Friends are just great, Journal. There's no substitute for them!

Chapter Eleven

The Big Tournament

Tuesday
8 P.M.

*A*nother week gone by. A good one, too! This was the week to really push the publicity for the big tournament that was held yesterday. Jon and I went down for one more interview with *The Collinsville Press.* And we actually rode our bikes out to the KCOL station for a half-hour interview right in the studio. I'd never been in a radio station before. The engineer gave us a tour of the entire place—it wasn't all that big, actually, but it was really neat. He explained all the different pieces of equipment. There's a lot to think about when you are a disc jockey. I had never realized before all that goes into a radio show.

We also got together and made posters to put in most of the downtown stores. Everybody was really cooperative.

We finished painting the park equipment on Saturday. It really looks great. The benches are white. The swing is bright blue. The slide is bright yellow. The monkey bars are red and the teeter-totter is orange. And the jungle gym is green. Kiersten took one look at the finished product and said, "A feast for my fun-loving eyes!" It couldn't have been said better!

A policeman told Mr. Clark Weaver that he had found four guys patrolling the park for us. Little did he know!

Labor Day was a warm sunny day. We were at the park at seven o'clock in the morning, our FF T-shirts on, ready to sell tournament scorecards. Aunt Beverly had helped me design the scorecards and she had them printed at Beck's, which advertises itself as "the fastest office staff in town." I like going in to Beck's—with all the stationery supplies and copy machines and pens and other writers' gear. It's a future-novelist's mini-heaven!

Anyway, some people were already in line at seven o'clock when we got there. And we were hopping all day. We finally closed up shop at eight o'clock in the evening—so that the last person could get through the course by nine o'clock. During the day, we kept a running tally of the scores to beat in each player category: under eight, eight to twelve, twelve to fourteen, fifteen to eighteen, eighteen to thirty, thirty to sixty-five, and over sixty-five. Kimber had painted a special Frisbee for each category winner and they were wonderful paintings! At nine o'clock sharp, we went over to the main stage of the Labor Day festival, where lots of people were still eating barbecue and pie, and we announced the winners. Six of the seven winners were there! The over-sixty-five winner wasn't present . . . but guess who it was? Mr. McGreggor! He beat out Grandpa Stone by one toss. I didn't even know that Grandpa Stone knew how to throw a Frisbee!

We also counted up the money. Given what we took in last week in the cannisters, and what people paid to enter the tournament . . . we took in a hundred and eighty dollars. Figuring that we still owe about twenty dollars for paint, we should have a hundred and sixty dollars more in our account. Wow! We *never* thought we'd make that much money. It will be fun to figure out what project to do next.

Libby and Julio played the course together and Julio almost won the fifteen-to-eighteen category—he missed it by just one toss. I definitely think there's something between those two. Libby has had two more swimming lessons without me . . . I'm going to have to ask her about that.

Aunt Beverly and Mr. Clark Weaver also played the course. They played in a foursome with Colleen, the friend of Aunt Beverly's who may open the new men's shop, and her boyfriend (at least I'm going to guess that's what he is)—his name is Jarrod. A nice guy. And the four of them seemed to be having fun. I've got to say though, Frisbee throwing is *not* Aunt Beverly's thing. She was funny to watch. The good part was that she was laughing at herself, too. Mr. Clark Weaver was *very* good. I thought he might win his category, but he never did turn in his scorecard. (He probably beat the socks off everybody and didn't want to embarrass the losers.) You can't convince me that Aunt Beverly and Mr. Clark Weaver aren't in love. There's just too much sparkle between them.

Jon and Kimber and Dennis and I manned the scorecard booth all day, taking turns for a lunch break. After Jon and I got our hot dogs at lunch, he asked me if I wanted to go to "Emily's Place" to eat. We decided not to go, since it was so far away, but the idea was neat. I'd almost forgotten about Emily's Place. I miss that secret little garden where I used to go have lunch every day during my first few weeks at Collinsville High. Jon's bringing it up made me feel nostalgic, like missing an old friend.

And then it hit me . . . I should ask Grandpa Stone about Emily! He's lived in Collinsville all his life, so he might know the story about Emily. I looked for Grandpa Stone all day, but I only saw him across the park. He and Mr. McGreggor had started playing the course while we were at lunch and I guess they finished when Jon and I went to get a pencil sharpener so people could sharpen the golf pencils we had made available to them for filling out their scorecards. (A sharpener was one detail we had forgotten.)

At the end of the night, after we had given out the awards, we all sat around a table together and ate the pie of our choice. There were lots of pies still uncut—in lots of different flavors. I think we each had at least two pieces. (Except for Libby, who was content to have just half a piece and a diet drink—such willpower!) Dennis actually had four pieces: one each of berry, peanut butter, peach, and chocolate. A very strange combination. I hope his stomach survives.

It was a good end to the summer. Which I can hardly believe is over. The tournament took so much of our concentration and energy that I've hardly had a minute to think about school starting. But sure enough, it does—tomorrow.

Isn't that appropriate? A new school year . . . and I'm ready to start a new journal book. I picked out one last week when a new shipment of blank books arrived in The Wonderful Life Shop. I wonder what its pages will hold. There's so much that could happen. . . .

I've got to find out about Libby's swimming

lessons with Julio, and how things are on that front.

And there's bound to be more happening between Aunt Beverly and Mr. Clark Weaver.

It sounds as if Trish is going to go to school at Collinsville High. She seems happy about that, especially because of Ford, I think.

I've *got* to talk to Grandpa Stone about Emily.

And besides all that, it will be my sophomore year! I feel ready, but who knows? In lots of ways, I'm still a new girl in town.

It's pretty amazing, though, all the changes that can happen in just one summer. I know people now. I feel a part of Collinsville. And best of all, I have friends I can really count on. So, here's to a new school year! May it be the best ever for all of us.

The End

Katelyn Weber
Collinsville

An excerpt from *Collinsville High*, Book Four in the Forever Friends series:

"So if we want to have prayer to start and end our FF Club meetings, we can't be a school club," I said, trying to get everything square in my mind—which was reeling. I couldn't fully believe what I was hearing. "But if we don't have prayer, we can be a school club?"

"Yes," Miss Kattenhorn said. "As long as you leave God out of your club, you can be an official school club."

If she had said it any other way, I might have been inclined to go along with what she said, but when she said those words "as long as you leave God out of your club," something inside of me really snapped. God has been a big part of our club. It's largely because of God that we *are* a club, and that we get along so well together as friends.

I was furious inside but I tried to be cool. Oh, how I wish Jon *had* been there with me! I said, "Well, Miss Kattenhorn, I guess we'll have to discuss this again as a club. I'm sorry I misunderstood what you said before. Now that I fully get the picture, we'll probably have to reconsider."

Watch for *Collinsville High* at a bookstore near you.